questionMark

Faryl

Copyright © 2016 Project 89 Media

All rights reserved.

ISBN: 0998388610

ISBN-13: 978-0998388618

Many people made this book happen
whether they knew it or not

Table of Contents

The Gadabout...1

I Saw the Fairies..13

Food..49

Eric Manchester Takes His Medicine.....................................68

Dreams..86

The Judgment Day to Come...114

The Gadabout

I do not know who I am.

It doesn't matter now. It never has. If I ever had a name, I had forgotten it long ago. Now, I only use the name legends have given me.

They call me the Gadabout.

No one can see me; I have no physical form. No one can hear me; I have no voice. No one can feel me; I have no presence, I have no touch. I am only a thought, an unfamiliar voice who whispers words strange and serene, soon to be forgotten in the stream of conscious. I come and go as time and destiny take me, drifting like the wind, aimless and helpless. Most of my hosts never know the difference.

Yes. "Hosts."

The legends call me an "energy vampire." To an extent, it is true: I feed off the human essence from some safe place in the mind, but never enough to weaken or kill. I will not lie, there have been accidents, but they are thankfully rare. I am a parasite, indeed, but not one without respect for life. I understand its value, how precious it really is. I understand that rebirth and growth are much more satisfying than a hearty fill.

I see life, and I dare not disturb it. It is beautiful, but only without me.

For centuries, I have traveled, created a chain of souls

throughout all time, linking humanity together, passing through the touch of fingertips. From every host, before I leave, I take wisdom, strength, and a tiny fragment of the soul, a memento. These make up my entire being, and I have only become stronger. However, I never use my power for anything but ritual; I have grown quite comfortable being an observer—as I have said, I dare not disturb the beauty of life. In the past, I had sometimes been tempted—and, in my foolish age, I had sometimes followed through—but in the end, I always saw that interference had grave consequences. I fear that you, who are listening to my tale, may suffer some of these consequences on my behalf.

However, I know you are troubled, and I hope that you wouldn't mind a companion, if only for a brief time.

I would parrot the wisdom of philosophers, scientists, writers, and artists, the wisest minds of all time, but I have gathered the courage to speak to you as myself.

You have the time and a clear mind, so I will tell you a tale of self and sacrifice. It begins in a time not long before yours, late on a rainy night. A man with empty pockets, soaking wet and chilling cold, had finally made it home to his young wife.

***

"James, what the hell happened? You were supposed to be home four hours ago!"

"I know. I'm sorry, Azumi."

"'Sorry'? What happened back there? You couldn't get a ride?" Azumi was about to help James take off his damp coat, but he waved her away and took it off himself. He felt a little better once the weight was off his shoulders, but it didn't help with the guilt.

"I didn't have enough for a taxi," James replied, before realizing what he had said.

"So you did lose." Azumi sighed, crossing her arms. "Could you make it any more obvious? God, James, you know you can't keep doing this. Eventually, I won't be able to give you any more money, especially if—"

"You think I don't know that? You think I haven't been trying?

Just give me one more chance."

"No, James. Not anymore. If you keep doing this, we're not going to have enough money for food."

"I know that."

"You know that, and yet you don't do anything about it. I can only be nice about this for so long before it's not worth it anymore. Before *you're* not worth it." With that, she turned around and headed toward the kitchen.

"Azumi!" James kept close behind her. "Y-You can't mean that. I mean, you know I'm doing all this for you, right?"

"Of course you are," she replied, looking over her shoulder. "That's what you tell me. That's what you've always told me. But for some reason, I don't believe you. I'm sorry, but it's gotten out of hand. I don't know what else to tell you, except to get your damn money somewhere else." She stopped in front of the kitchen sink. "I love you, but I don't love you enough to let you throw away my inheritance."

"It's not like that."

"Then, enlighten me. What *is* it like?" Azumi turned to face him. "Because my way of getting money back is not losing it in the first place, keeping it in the bank instead of giving it to bums like you. I've appeased you all these years, James. I've let you borrow money from me so you can go play cards, and you keep telling me you'll pay me back. You'll pay me back, you'll pay me back, you'll pay me back, and yet every night, you show up without so much as lint in your pocket. I'm sorry, James, but I can't do this anymore. Either get a job or have a garage sale, just find some way to pay me back so we don't go broke. Now, I'm going to make dinner," she added mechanically, turning her back to him once again. "I'll call you when it's done."

James was about to respond, but he thought better of it. She had always told him to go get a "real" job instead of spending his time gambling, but she couldn't understand the fact that there was nothing—absolutely nothing—useful he could do. He had never been able to get through college, and it was impossible for him to get a job no matter how much he prepared for his interviews, almost as if fate wanted to keep him rooted to the spot. The only thing he had going for him was his luck, or so he thought. James tried to shake the thought out of his head. Maybe it was all rigged, like a cheap carnival game that seemed so simple, but the bottles normally nailed to the pedestal were now made out of steel. And on the other side of that impossible task, Azumi's love. At this point, James had spent so much time on that one game, it would have been more worthwhile to just buy out the whole damn carnival.

But he was going to keep playing, even though he knew it wasn't fair. He would win, and he would make those cheating bastards pay. Even if he had to take the money off their dead bodies...

James made his way to the living room and threw himself onto the couch, shivering a little. The tension melted away, and he became limp the moment his body hit the cushions. Suddenly, his mind told him to relax. It sounded like a voice in his head, but maybe that was just his imagination. Just his body telling him to skip everything else and go to bed because this night needed to be over as soon as possible. James wasn't about to argue with that logic. He closed his eyes, and within moments, he dozed off.

*

Fascinating. As I had my fill, I searched through James' mind. As it turned out, his luck *was* irreparably terrible; there was nothing he could do, nothing that could happen, no possible way he could win back the money his wife had loaned him. People like him, though they made ideal hosts, made horrible gamblers, as I have discovered many times throughout the course of history. People like him, they *projected* their emotions: anger, anxiety, depression, fear ... they could all be sensed from a world away. James wouldn't be able to contain himself long enough to avenge his losses. This was a battle he couldn't win.

And yet ... his love, his concern for his wife was genuine—or, at least, that's what he believed. Even when she no longer believed in him, he believed in himself for her sake. He was still going to try, even though it would inevitably do more harm than good. Poor man. He earned his sleep for the night.

But there was something else about this encounter, too, something I couldn't shake. From the moment James had grabbed his companion's wrist out of frustration during his poker game to when he had gone to sleep just a few moments ago, I was seeing through his eyes and letting his mental processes course through my being as if he and I were one. For that time, I had lost myself within him, but something seemed to have pulled me from my trance prematurely.

It was a ... feeling of some kind.

Nothing from James' mind, I was sure of that. At that point, I knew him well enough to judge that the feeling was ... out of character. It was unusual, even for me. Nothing like this had ever happened to me before, not once throughout all time. Had it been from within ... myself? Impossible—very rarely did I have thoughts of my own, only recollections of past experiences and echoes of words from other souls.

Perhaps there is a Gadabout within myself, one I am unaware of as my hosts are unaware of me, and one who had chosen only now to speak and only had one word to say:

Azumi.

Looking at her, listening to her speak, feeling James' raging emotions coursing through him and through me like nipping sparks, it gave me a feeling within myself, one so powerful it broke my trance for a time, and I remembered that we were two beings in one mind. This was nothing like what James felt for her. This was ...

Many of my wiser hosts have found definitions for love. According to them, there were several different kinds: love that has stayed strong over time, flickered like a flame stroked by wind, gone out, succumbed to the storm. But then there was *new* love: the kind of love, I've heard, that sets the soul aflame, gives new and sudden meaning to life, that keeps a man awake for many nights be it from ecstasy or crippling depression. Was this what was happening to me?

For once, I didn't have an answer.

In the past, I always had something to offer, an adage from a soul long gone to share with my troubled host. But not once had I ever had to console *myself*. How would I? Giving myself wisdom was useless; there was nothing within my being I didn't already know. I searched through my knowledge, I searched within myself, but it was all just *words*: concatenations of phonetic sounds, coordinated lines and curves. None of it could help me now.

I never liked to think about the fact that I had the power to fully possess a human body. I could never bring myself to use it. It would mean that I would fully consume the soul and its energy, giving it a fate that, to me, was far worse than the death of its shell. But as I was now, I was dependent on James' whims. If he continued to make Azumi suffer, albeit unintentionally, I would be helpless. At the very idea, I found myself engulfed in ... sadness. *Me*, completely independent of my host, who at the time was sleeping peacefully. I found myself wanting—*desperately* wanting—a way to comfort her, if and when James would try his luck again. I found myself wanting to *be* with her, not only as a temporary companion, not only as a guest in her mind, but ...

In theory, I could stay with James and be able to see Azumi for a little while longer. However, I couldn't turn a blind eye to the inevitable. It had happened too many times before, and for lesser reasons than this: I had lost track of time, or I couldn't find another host, something along those lines, but never this. Never anything like this.

And why? Why Azumi, and why now? What was it about her presence that drew me to her, that made me think about her more than a thought should? The combination of physical elements that gave her her beauty—her porcelain face, her almond eyes, her raven hair, her musical voice— was that what drew me? Did the stars or planets align in my favor?

Or was it *my* power? Was I finally strong enough to become something ... more? Did I have enough fragments to become a whole? I didn't want to think about that. I didn't want to think about having that kind of power. I wouldn't be able to trust myself. I would be like James, thinking I could do more than I could, doing more damage than ... I couldn't use my power.

But what about Azumi?

I couldn't communicate with her. Even if we did share a mind, I wouldn't know what to say. My thoughts and opinions were those from the chain of humanity I had left behind. Not once had *I* ever said anything; it had always been from this person or that, whom I had known before. I had never had a true conversation, one between the host and myself, and even if I had tried, no one would think to respond. But could I try now? If I managed to speak to Azumi in some way, would she accept me? Or would she be afraid of me? Probably. Why did it even occur to me, if I knew it wasn't going to work?

All these worries were new to me. It made me ... nervous. I didn't know what to think. I didn't know what to say, if I should say anything at all, or even if I *could*. I didn't know what to do. I tried to call upon my wisdom again, but still, no words could help me. For the first time, I found myself struggling to make a decision.

... No.

For the first time, I found myself *having* to make a decision.

*

I had decided to stay with James for the time being. I did it to give myself more time to think, or, at least, that's what I kept telling myself.

But I was driven by *wants*. I wanted to see Azumi. I wanted to hear her voice from within someone she loved, if only to pretend it was me, myself, and not my host. The sensation of "pretending," it was also something I had never felt before. The act of deceiving myself of reality, as I had deceived others in the past, was strange and yet satisfying at the same time. Was this the appeal of plays and literature, of fiction? To escape from reality itself and yet never move? As I absorbed myself in the facade, as James woke up in the morning and went about his day, I had plenty of opportunities to move on to my next host and leave James and Azumi behind, to let them become only another way station on my travels across eternity. But I refused. I stayed and I unintentionally began to draw more energy from him, even after I had already had my fill. I couldn't help it.

I hadn't realized how much damage I had done until two days

later when James woke up ... or, at least, when he tried. His pulse was slower. His thoughts were less rapid. His energy flow was less a raging river and more an ambling creek. He could barely speak. He could barely move. He only drifted in and out of sleep, numb to the world around him.

And yet, I was the strongest I had been in ages. When had I ever felt like this? The power I had, combined with what I was afraid I was capable of ...

I had a *chance*.

I knew that if I took enough of his energy—enough to kill him—then I would be powerful enough to take his body for myself. Would she know the difference? Azumi would look at me the same way, and I would love her more than James ever ...

No. I couldn't say that. I knew perfectly well how much he loved her. He had loved her enough to keep beating his head into a brick wall for a feeble chance at forgiveness, and me? I could never match that.

But wouldn't it be better if James died? She had been close to leaving him, anyway. If he suddenly began treating her better and straightening his life ...

It didn't matter what kind of person he was or what he did with his life. He was always significant to someone, and that someone was Azumi.

Azumi, who found him in his bedroom after he had slept in later than usual. Azumi, who called doctors and paid them with the money that James would have gambled away. Azumi, who urged them to keep looking for a physical cause even when they said James' coma was inexplicable. Azumi, who sat at his bedside whenever she could and talked to him, hoping there was a slight chance that he would respond to her. Azumi, who stayed with him ...

I felt terrible, even though I knew this was my chance. He only had a little bit of life left, and if I took that, then I could have his body. I could end my travels here, once and for all.

Just a few more hours, and then for the first time, I could open my eyes.

But I heard her crying. I heard her say his name. I felt her grab his hand. She held it tight, a new contender in the tug-of-war for his life.

I knew how much he loved her. How much she loved him. Despite everything he had done in the past, she had still forgiven him. I knew from looking through James' memories that she had encouraged him to better himself, but it had never worked out. He had never *let* it work out. Should he have another chance? I was running out of time to say yes, but it was the only answer I could give.

He was the one Azumi loved, not me. She would have been able to tell the difference immediately. She would have most likely resented me; she would have known that I was the one who had killed him in the end. She would never forgive me.

It would have been all for nothing.

All life is beautiful, but only without me.

She was still holding his hand.

I knew what I had to do. I knew what I was giving up. I didn't care.

I let go.

*

Azumi had only looked away for a second, but when she focused on James again, she saw that the color was returning to his skin, and his breathing became more pronounced. She didn't know why or how it had happened—hell, no one knew what had put him in the coma to begin with—but whatever it was, it had been a miracle. The anxiety and fear melted away, and joyful tears streamed down her cheeks as she embraced him, talked to him, tried to coax him back into the land of the living.

Eventually, he came back, only to find a message left for him deep in his subconscious:

Listen to her. You are lucky to have her. I have given you another chance. Do not waste it.

*

Hello, Azumi.

What? Where am I? Who are you?

Please, don't be afraid. I'm not here to hurt you.

Who are you?

I am a visitor ... a visitor, inside your mind. Your dreams are the only way I can ... communicate with you.

What are you talking about? How—?! Who are you? What are you?

I know it's strange. It's strange to me, too. I would explain everything—believe me, I would—but we don't have much time.

You haven't even told me who you are.

It's ... I ... I don't know if ...

Show yourself!

... I can't do that.

Why?

I ... It's hard to ... Hard to explain. Really, I ...

...

... Never mind, I shouldn't have even ...

What?

... No ... I'm here now. I should just ... say it.

Say what? What are you talking about?

Azumi, I ... I need to ... apologize.

For what? What did you do?

... I-I need to ... apologize about ... about your husband.

James? What do you know about him? Wh-what did you do to him? Who are you?

Azumi, I am a ... parasite. A parasite of the ... the mind.

Parasite? What are you—? That was you? ... You tried to kill him—why? What did he do? What did I do?

It's ... It's difficult ... I don't really ... There was no ... There was no reason, not that you can comprehend, but ... please, please, don't be afraid, please don't think about me like that—

How else can I? You tried to kill him! You almost killed him! And for no reason—Why? Tell me!

Yes, I ... I won't deny that, but ... I ... I didn't mean it.

... You didn't mean it.

... Yes.

How exactly does that work?

... I don't know.

You don't know.

... Yes.

I can't believe this. Well, what do you know?

I know that ... Never mind. I ... I shouldn't have done this. I-I shouldn't have said anything. I shouldn't have ...

Attempted murder? If you have the balls, whatever you are, to apologize, then maybe you could've had a little more common sense!

... I shouldn't have spoken to you. This was a ... a bad idea. It won't make much of a difference.

Why? Are you going to kill me, too? Is that why you're here?

No, it's ... it's not. Azumi, I don't ... I don't want to do that. I wouldn't dream of doing it.

And why's that?

Because ... Because ... I ... I don't know how to say this. It's ... I ... Never mind.

Just get it over with.

Azumi, I ... I ...

...

...

...

... I love you.

...

...

... *What?*

There. I said it. I'm sorry. That's why ... That's why I didn't leave, even though ... I'm sorry.

... *I don't understand.*

I knew you wouldn't. Nothing like this has ... has ever happened to you before. And nothing like this has ever happened to me before, either. But please, let me explain.

... *I'm listening.*

I was ... only planning to stay inside your husband's mind for a short time. I go, I ... feed a little, and then I ... move on. That's the way I've always done it. But when I saw you through his eyes ... when I saw you, I ... I can't explain what happened. Not with a thousand years of wisdom. I ... I wanted to see you all the time, not just for a few days. I wanted you to ... know me, talk to me, look at me. That was the only time I wanted a ... a body of my own.

So you were able to ... to ... suck his soul out, or ...?

N-n-n-no, it ... it doesn't work like that. It would ... it would take all night to explain, but ... I-I guess part of it does ... work that way. I-I mean, I could have had a body, a physical body, and then, I could have—N-no, I mean ...

You could have used his?

Well, no, I ... I-I mean ... yes, I could have ... taken it, and ... you wouldn't have ... known the difference.

You were going to steal it?

... In a sense. After I ... killed him.

So you think that almost killing him is better? Is that what you're saying?

Yes! Because ... because you still have him. He'll live. He'll recover in a few weeks, and it'll be like this never happened; he'll be just as healthy if not healthier than before. You care about him. You've shown that, and ... and that's why I let him live. Because I couldn't kill him. It wouldn't have been right.

So what now?

I know that ... after tonight, you'll ... you'll never hear from me again ...You have earned that leisure. You will ... move on, as I will, and ... and hopefully, your relationship will grow stronger because of this. Before I left him, I ... I encouraged him to find his talents—I searched through his mind, he has some even he doesn't know. As far as ... As far as what will happen to you ... your sadness and fear will all be gone by the morning. It is part of my talent. You will have pleasant dreams for the rest of the night, and more than likely ... you will forget you ever met me. Perhaps it is better this way. Until we meet again, if ever ... goodbye, and know that ... that you are loved here on this earth and beyond.

I Saw the Fairies

"Jason! Jason!"

Pari ran into the house and up the stairs to her brother's bedroom. Her pink, sparkly Converse tracked mud all over the floor, but she didn't care. She knew what she had seen.

She stopped in front of Jason's bedroom and pounded on the door. She didn't care what she was interrupting; no grown-up stuff could be more important than this.

"Jason! Jason! JASON!"

Jason, sole companion and guardian of his eight-year-old sister, opened the door and leaned against the doorframe, clinging to it with one hand as if for dear life.

"Whaddiyawan?" he asked, rubbing his eyes with his free hand.

Jason was would be turning twenty-five in a few days. Seven years ago, when he was a freshman in college, he had gotten the news that his parents and two of his siblings had disappeared, leaving him to take care of Pari. Unable to afford an apartment close to campus that would allow him to bring Pari as well, he moved back to their parents' old house and regularly made the three-hour commute back and forth to class. Now, the last of his inheritance (and the fruits of several minimum wage jobs) was about to run out, and while Pari was getting old enough to understand their situation, the balance between being a parent and a student had not gotten any easier.

"It's important," Pari said as soon as he could actually focus on her. "It's really, *really* important. You need to hear this."

"Whaddisit?" He shook his head a little, trying to keep himself awake enough to listen to what Pari had to say.

"I saw them again."

Was it possible for kids her age to be this serious? Especially when talking about *this*? Jason sighed. He gradually shifted from rubbing his eyes to rubbing his temples to running his fingers through his shaggy hair. He knew what she was talking about, but he felt obligated to ask anyway. "Who'd you see?"

"The fairies."

Jason let his eyes close, and he fell limp against the doorframe. He would have rolled his eyes at her instead, but he knew it would hurt her feelings, and God knew how much *that* had happened every time she brought this up.

"The fairies in the old garden," Pari continued, "I saw them, Jason. I keep seeing them. I think they're watching me."

They had to go through this. *Every. Single. Damn. Time.* He could have sworn it was like rehearsing lines for a school play or bad sitcom. None of it really mattered, except to cue the invisible "LAUGHTER" sign above them.

"They're watching you."

"Uh-huh, and I figured out why. Y'know why, Jason?"

"Hit me."

"I think I'm a changeling. Y'know what that is, Jason?"

Jason considered stopping her in her tracks, considered telling her to stop talking about it or else he'd send her to her room or whatever real parents did. However, he was half-asleep, so the only thing he felt like doing was obliging her. For probably the fifteenth time that month.

"Go ahead."

"The fairies, they—they have a baby, and then they switch it out with a-a human baby—"

"Uh-huh."

"And then the fairy baby is raised by the people, and then the fairy doesn't know that she's a fairy until a certain age when they come to get her, and—"

"And how do you know all this? You learn about it in school?"

"*They* told me."

"... So, they talk to you, too?"

"Uh-huh. They tell me all kinds of things."

"Like, uh, like what? What do you guys talk about? Unicorns?"

Pari giggled. "No, silly. Everyone knows unicorns aren't real."

Jason sighed. There was nothing he could really say to that. "Look, we'll talk about this later. I don't feel like having an argument with you right now. I just want to go back to sleep. I just want to go to sleep and forget that fairies exist—"

"So you do think they exist!"

"I never said ...! I didn't ...Ugh, whatever. I don't want to hear any more about this."

With that, Jason retreated into his room, shut the door, and collapsed onto the bed before Pari could get another word out.

"Make yourself dinner," he slurred through his pillow, hoping that his laziness would pay off and that Pari could hear him from the other side of the door.

*

"Jason? Are you awake?"

That night, Pari knocked on the bedroom door again, although with much less ferocity than before. No response. When she invited herself in and noticed that Jason was still asleep, she tiptoed to the bed and gently tapped his shoulder.

"Jason? Jason?"

No response. She started to shake him gently.

"Jason? Jason? Hey, Jason."

Jason groaned, rolling over to face her as he half-opened his eyes.

"Hunh? Wha? Whatimeizzit?"

"It's about ten."

"Ugh, what? Awwfff—" He was about to say what was on his mind when he remembered Pari's presence. He'd gotten surprisingly used to holding back his language around her. "Shouldn't you be in bed by now?"

"I saw the fairies again."

"I told you, I don't want to hear about it."

"No, this is important. You *need* to hear this."

"You said that the last time."

"No, I mean it this time."

"So you didn't mean it last time?" He managed a sly smirk, although he was too drowsy to tell if anything was actually funny.

But Pari wasn't laughing. "They said to apologize to you. They said I was rude, and that a changeling should be more respectful."

Jason sighed and rolled over again so his back was to Pari. "God, Pari, not this bull again. You mean to tell me—"

"They also told me that the human family can see them, too, but only if they really, really want to. So you have to really, really want to in order to see them."

Jason hesitated, before propping his pillow and sitting up. "Let me guess, I have to clap my hands and believe *reeeeeeeal* hard?" He clapped his hands a few times for emphasis.

Pari scowled. "Shut up. I'm serious."

"So am I." Jason chuckled, feeling a little more awake. "I wanna know." When he noticed that Pari didn't even crack a smile, Jason sighed. She really was taking this seriously, wasn't she? "Look, I'm sorry. But we've been through this a million times. There's no such thing as fairies. Every time you 'see' them, you tell me to go out there, and when I do, they're conveniently gone. Just like the monster under your bed and the boogieman in your closet. You got over that, so you think you could get over this?"

"It's not something to 'get over,'" Pari muttered. "I can prove they're real. And you have to *want* me to prove they're real."

"Jesus, Pari, what kind of—?" Jason huffed and ran his fingers through his hair, almost pulling it out of his scalp. "I'm not going to win this, am I?" he muttered. He looked over at Pari again. "Fine. I'm awake now, anyway. But here's the deal: I'll go out there, and I'm gonna 'want' to see them as much as I can. But when—yeah, I said 'when'—*when* they're not there, will you try not to be so upset about it? We'll, uh, I dunno, we'll go out for ice cream tomorrow, I guess. You still like ice cream, Batman?"

"Vanilla with chocolate sprinkles," Pari muttered, trying as hard as she could to keep her "serious" face.

"Yeah, that's what I thought. Okay, squirt, gimme a few minutes to get dressed, and I'll meet you out there."

Pari started to leave the room, but then she turned around and asked, "If you see that they're real, will you stop making fun of me about it?"

Jason chuckled. She was starting to sound like him.

"Sure."

*

This was the last time, Jason told himself. This was the last time he was going to play along with Pari's stupid fairy games. Had he ever been this crazy as a kid? He didn't remember very much of his childhood, only that every so often, he would go alone into the big forest by the middle school, and ... he never remembered much of what happened there, only that he *went*. Bella and Danny had never played there, but Pari, when she was old enough, had found it on her own and played there ever since.

Then, Jason remembered that his sister's obsession with the "fairies" had begun soon after she started going to the forest. Was that just a coincidence, or was the forest involved somehow? Why did it make her take this fairy business so seriously? Was that why Pari was the only one who had this obsession? Did it have anything to do with his lack of memory of the forest itself? Was it ...?

Soon, Jason found himself unconsciously following through with his part of the deal. He found himself *wanting* ... answers. He wanted to know what happened. He wanted to be able to put all the pieces together, to fill the holes that needed to be filled. And if "magic" of some kind was going to explain everything, then that was all he wanted for—

Was this really what Pari was doing to him? What *life* was doing to him? Had it all gone so downhill that he was resorting to kid stuff—little girl stuff, at that—to find closure? To find answers? Alcohol was a more logical method. Despite his growing doubts, though, Jason tried his best to keep "believing," especially when he and Pari sat cross-legged at the edge of the garden. A small part of him *wanted* to be surprised, to be proven wrong, but the rest of him knew the truth: that Pari was just wasting his time.

"This is where I saw them earlier today," Pari said. "You can see them better at night because they glow like fireflies."

"How do you know they *aren't*?" He could see tiny lights flickering in the distance, but he knew they were just fireflies ... right?

"They're *brighter* than fireflies, duh! Just watch. You'll be able to tell when you see them."

They watched, but nothing came. There was an occasional flicker of light that was brighter than usual, much to Pari's excitement and (although he was reluctant to admit it) Jason's curiosity, but it had turned out to be just a firefly every time. After about fifteen minutes of Pari insisting that the fairies were just hiding or playing jokes, Jason sighed and stood up.

"Now do you understand?"

"*No!*" she yelled, echoing through the otherwise still night. She jumped to her feet as well. "They *have* to be here! They promised they would come, they *promised*! You lied to me, Jason! You said you were going to *want* to see them!"

"Pari!" Jason snapped. The last thing he wanted to do was admit she was right. "Pari, remember what *you* promised? You said you wouldn't be upset about those stupid fairies if we didn't see any out here. Remember that? And, look, we didn't see any, just like I said. Now, stop being a little brat and let's go inside."

"They're not stupid! *You're* stupid!" Pari shouted, but after a moment, she began to slump, her anger fading into disappointment. "Okay. I'm sorry, Jason."

"I'm sorry, too," Jason replied. "It's just that you need to keep your promises, okay? When you say you're gonna do something, you gotta do it. Now, let's go inside, you need to get to bed."

*

Later that night, Jason was working on an overdue assignment when he heard glass breaking and Pari screaming.

Oh, shit! On impulse, Jason grabbed the first thing he could find—a two-liter of soda that he had just opened and taken a large swig of only a few minutes ago—and ran downstairs.

Someone had broken into the house. Or maybe Pari had just broken something by accident. No, Pari had been in bed, he knew that for a fact, so why was she downstairs? Because someone had broken into the house? Because she was a hostage? Oh, God, what would he do then? He needed to be calm, that was the first thing he needed to do. He needed to be levelheaded enough in order to take care of the problem, even if Pari was being held hostage. The police. If someone had really broken into the house, he needed to call the police somehow. Pari could call the police while Jason fought off whoever had broken in.

Unless Pari didn't *want* to.

His train of thought had somehow returned to the topic of fairies. To the whole "changeling" thing that Pari always went on about. What if they were real? No, what if they *weren't* real, and whoever had broken into the house had convinced Pari that they were? They would have a very good reason to kidnap her because she was a "changeling." They were going to kidnap her, take her to some abandoned warehouse somewhere, and while she'd still be stuck in her own personal fantasyland, they'd try to get a ransom or, worse, they'd …

Jason tiptoed into the living room, holding the two-liter like a heavy, stubby baseball bat, but he stumbled as he saw Pari standing next to a broken vase. He normally would have freaked out, yelled at her, said something about how that vase had belonged to their parents and how she shouldn't have been so careless. However, Jason was willing to ignore the broken antique because behind Pari was a seven-foot-tall, thin woman with long, white hair wearing a gown made of pure silver.

Jason restrained himself from making any sudden movements. He didn't want to provoke the intruder in any way that would cause her to harm him or Pari. Not to mention she looked … familiar. He didn't want to dwell on that for too long, though, because there were more important things to worry about.

"Who are you?" he asked, forcing a calm tone, fully prepared to smack a bitch with a two-liter if necessary. "What are you doing in my house?"

"She's one of the fairies," Pari said. "The ones I've been telling you about."

"Pari," Jason hissed through gritted teeth, "what did I tell you? There's no such thing."

"But she said she's come for the changeling, Jason. She wants me."

Oh, God. This was the warehouse outcome, wasn't it? Jason narrowed his eyes; no, that wasn't going to happen.

"Really?" Jason turned to the intruder. "Is that what you told her? You know, you really should be ashamed of yourself, lying to a little girl like that. That is *low*. Look, if you want money, I can get it for you. If you want to kill someone, kill me. I'm sure we can arrange something. But, please, for the love of God, just leave her alone. She didn't do anything, she doesn't deserve whatever you're trying to do to her. She's just a kid, okay? Stop trying to brainwash her."

"I don't intend to brainwash her." *That voice* … Her voice was like the jingling of a small bell, but an old and rusty one, the kind that more clanked and clunked than made a pleasant sound. There was definitely a kind of sweetness in her voice, but it—she—had obviously gone through some wear and tear. But why did he think it was so familiar?

Regardless, Jason needed to defend himself and Pari. "Don't play games with me, you sick bitch. I know you only put this together just to trick her into going with you without a fight. It's not going to work."

"I can assure you this is no trick. Please, let me prove to you—"

"I don't want 'proof.' I've had enough 'proof' for tonight. What I *want* is for you to leave, or I'm going to call the pol—"

However, Jason never got a chance to finish, as a sudden gust of wind rippled from the woman's body, sending antiques flying around and across the room and shifting furniture from one end to the other. Amid the chaos, wings not unlike a butterfly's burst from the woman's back and created another larger gust with a force strong enough to knock Jason off his feet, causing the two-liter to fly from his hands and explode on the ground, sending sticky, caffeinated syrup everywhere.

However, that was the least of Jason's problems right now.

When everything had settled down, broken glass was everywhere. About a quarter of the room was covered in soda. The furniture had been shifted and shuffled around the room like one of those annoying slide-puzzles. And in the center of it all ... a fairy. A damn fairy.

Or the intruder had spent thousands on props and effects, all to win the affection of this one little girl. In that case, this was one desperate sicko.

"Did you see that, Jason? Did you see it? A real fairy! I told you! I told you they were real!" Pari shouted, but Jason wasn't paying attention.

"Oh, God," he muttered, still unable to take his eyes off the ... fairy. "Oh, God, what the ... the hell did I just ...?"

The fairy glanced around at the mess, before waving her hand. Before Jason could even think to ask what she was doing, everything that had been broken was suddenly fixed and returned to its proper place. The furniture was back where it should have been, and there was even a fresh two-liter of the same soda that had exploded, all traces of which seemed to have disappeared as well. Everything was as if that little fireworks show had never happened.

"So," the fairy asked, "do you have the proof you need?"

Jason searched his mind for some kind of logical explanation, something that would be able to justify the idea of this woman being a desperate and filthy rich pedophile. However, there was nothing. Smoke and mirrors couldn't replace priceless antiques, move furniture around, and then put it right back where it had been before; it couldn't un-soda-stain an entire room and give a complimentary replacement two-liter right along with it.

"Look," Jason started once he was able to speak coherently, "I have no idea what the hell just happened, but ... damn." Propping himself up against the couch, which was now back in its rightful place, Jason managed a slow clap. "I gotta say, I'm impressed. You ...You must have put a lot of money into that. I mean ...

damn." His applause ended. "That being said, though, you're still not taking her. Here's the deal—" He decided to give a condensed version of "the deal" before the fairy could try anything else. "—you leave, you never show your face here again, and I don't call the police. We forget this ever happened, j-just stay away from my sister, okay? She's not going with you. We clear on this?"

"Yes." Her calm monotone suggested that she hadn't taken him seriously from the beginning, but Jason tried not to let that bother him. "We are 'clear.'" But she didn't budge, the slow, mesmerizing movement of her wings (back and forth, back and forth, back and forth ...) creating a gentle breeze around them.

"Look, what did I just say?" Jason stood up and brandished the new two-liter. "Get out of here! You're not taking her. She's not the one you want."

The fairy smirked. "You're right. She's not the one I want."

Jason, startled, was about to follow up with, "These aren't the droids you're looking for" when Pari cut in.

"But ... But ... you said *I* was the changeling!"

"I never said that. I only said there was a changeling *here*. I didn't say it was you." The fairy's monotone had become condescending, and she ignored Pari's shrill whining.

"Wait." At this revelation, Jason's mind completely shut down. He needed at least a few minutes to process the strange turn of events. "So you mean ... if she's not who you're looking for, then who ...?" After a moment: "Oh, come on! What—?!"

The fairy chuckled, although it was flat with disappointment. "You are your father's child," she said, before adding as though to make herself feel better, "You are so brave."

As the fairy approached him, Jason backed against the wall, still holding the two-liter in front of him like a sword. "This doesn't make any sense. This doesn't make any sense at all. Why would I be—? Who—? What the hell—? What—? This makes no sense. This makes *no* frickin' sense."

The fairy stood in front of him, and he looked up at her with shuddering breaths.

"Well, that's because," she started as she gently placed the tips of her fingers on his forehead, "there are some pieces missing."

*

He was playing out in the park by the Big Kid School. He had a big, white ball that he loved to play with, loved to toss up into the air and try to catch, try to see how high he could toss it, try to see how many times in a row he could catch it. Whenever he threw it up too far, he would chase it down and grab it before throwing it up into the air again. It was a lot of fun. Some other kids were at the playground nearby, laughing and screaming, but Jason was so absorbed in his little game that he didn't realize it was taking him farther and farther away from everyone else. Mommy was busy; she'd found a friend of hers, ugly cootie-bug Mindy Hammond's mommy, and was too busy talking to watch him. But Jason kept playing.

He had wandered into the scary forest, still throwing the ball and trying to catch it, before he realized where he was and how far away he was from Mommy. The forest! Some of the grown-ups said there were monsters here, and that some people had dee-eye-ee-dee here. Now no longer caring about what happened to his favorite ball, Jason curled up against a big tree and cried. He didn't know what was going to happen to him now—were the monsters going to eat him? Was he going to die here? Would the animals save him and take him in, like in The Jungle Book? Or was he just going to be so scared he would pee his pants and then everyone else would laugh at him? He hoped Mommy would find him soon.

Jason was crying so much he had almost missed the sound of leaves rustling, branches snapping, someone coming. He looked up to see a tall, nice-looking lady kneeling down in front of him. She had long, white hair, and she was wearing a long dress that looked like it was made out of a bazillion shiny beads.

"Don't be afraid, little one," she said. She had found his ball! After a few moments, he took it and held it tight against his chest, never wanting to lose it ever again. Then, the lady stood up and said, "I'll help you find your way back."

Not knowing what else to do, Jason trusted her, and he followed her to the edge of the forest, back to the park, where Mommy was calling for him.

"*Someday,*" he thought he heard the Shiny Lady say as he ran off.

When he ran back to her, Mommy wrapped him up in a big hug, before asking where he had been.

"*I was in the woods,*" Jason said. "*I got lost. But the Shiny Lady helped me.*"

"*What shiny lady?*" his mother asked, frowning.

Jason turned around and was about to point to where the Shiny Lady had been standing, but she was gone.

Years passed. It was almost time for Jason to go to the Big Kid School, what the grown-ups called "middle school." He barely remembered that incident in preschool with the Shiny Lady, but he still thought it was worth investigating. No one he had told about the incident knew what he was talking about, or even believed him. They all thought he was just making it up, even when he was far too old to have "imaginary friends". Maybe, if he saw her again, he'd be able to get some pictures or something, just to show people he wasn't lying.

Jason couldn't explain why he didn't just forget the whole incident after kindergarten. It probably had something to do with the fact that he had never seen anyone like her before, and he hadn't seen anyone like her since. Not to mention he remembered her so <u>vividly</u>, even though he hadn't seen her for years. He could describe her face, her hair, her gown to the tiniest detail, and she just wouldn't leave his mind. There was some nagging part of his brain that told him she lived in the forest and never left there, so he would often go and investigate.

He usually told Mom that he spent the time after school practicing basketball with his friends, just so she wouldn't be worried about him. Those rumors about people going into the forest and never coming out hadn't let up, and Mom would probably ground him if she found out he had been hanging out here, "just asking for trouble." However, Jason knew he wouldn't have anything to worry about. After all, these days, Mom was more worried about baby Bella, which left him free to do pretty much whatever he wanted as long as he b.s.'d an excuse (he had heard one of the "middle school" kids say it, but he didn't know exactly what it meant). It was a plus to having a baby sister, he *guessed.*

Today, like every other day after school, Jason walked along the faint path of the forest, his bookbag lazily over his shoulder. He looked around for any sign of a Shiny Lady, but there was none. He decided to go deeper into the forest, wondering exactly how far he had wandered when ... he'd only been a little older than Bella, he reflected. Then, he thought: when did a baby become a kid? Three? Four? He'd probably find out when he was older when he was in middle school—or even high school!

He'd probably been considered a kid back then, Jason concluded after a moment of thinking, since he had been in preschool at the time, and babies couldn't go to school of any kind. Bella wasn't in school yet, but Mom always said it was never too early to prepare.

Jason looked around. How did he get here? He was lost—again! He had gotten lost many times before on "investigations" like this, and most of the time, he never remembered anything other than going home later that night. He never knew if he had actually found the Shiny Lady or if he just kept wandering around for hours until he found his way out. Was the same thing going to happen here? Jason hoped not. He was going to try, no matter how hard it was, to remember this investigation, just so he knew it could be done. Nothing was going to make him forget this time.

As soon as that thought occurred to him, Jason saw it: in a small glade off the path, a tall figure sat on a low tree branch, brushing her long, white hair and singing in a language he couldn't understand. A closer look at her clothing and he knew—this was the Shiny Lady! She looked exactly as Jason remembered, but she was even more beautiful than he had ever imagined. He must have gotten too close because the Shiny Lady heard his clumsy movements and looked in his direction. She jumped off the branch and landed effortlessly on the ground, before walking toward him as if her bare feet were on clouds.

"You came back to me," the Shiny Lady said, standing in front of him. She smiled. "I never told you how much you've grown. You've grown quite a lot. If only—" She cut herself off, clearly wanting to say more but forcing herself to only smile

apologetically at him. "I'm sorry, my darling," she continued, gently placing her fingertips on his forehead, "but you're not ready yet."

Then, Jason was back at the edge of the forest as if he had never explored in the first place. The sun was about to set, so he headed straight home, hoping Mom wouldn't ask too many questions. He had forgotten.

*

"Th-That couldn't have been you. Or—you couldn't be her, whatever … This doesn't make any sense. The Shiny Lady, she—she's not real. I was just seeing things, that's all. I-I was just a kid then. I made stuff up, big deal. How did you even—? I've never seen you before in my life."

"I took away your memory of our encounters to protect you," the fairy explained, taking a few steps back so Jason could move, "but you always managed to return. You finally gave up when you were thirteen."

"… How do you know all this? I never told anyone that. L-look, you're creeping me out, okay? I don't care who you are or what you are, just …"

"You saw them when you were little, too?"

"No," Jason replied, sharply turning to Pari. "No, I didn't."

"Just one," the fairy corrected him. "All he was allowed to see."

Jason turned his attention back to the fairy. "Look, you're not the Shiny Lady. The Shiny Lady's not real, okay? So stop trying to tell me she is. I've moved on."

The fairy sighed. "I was afraid this would happen. It's a common consequence of missing the coming-of-age."

"What? What are you talking about?" Jason asked.

"You've become, for lack of a better term, too human."

"I don't know what you're talking about! I've *always* been human."

"*This* is what I'm talking about. You've become so rooted in your life that there's no room for change. So many human beliefs forced upon you, you forget who you really are, or—" The fairy cut herself off and sighed. "Or it's just me getting ahead of myself. I'm sorry for your confusion. Please, just give me one day, and you'll have all the answers you need. I'll even let you meet your real father. Please, give me this chance."

" ... You really want me to go with you."

"I promise," the fairy replied, almost in desperation, "that nothing will happen to you. If you do get hurt, or if one of us hurts you in any way, you are no longer obligated to stay. You would be free to leave, and you would never see or hear from us again."

Jason was about to accept, but there was still one nagging question in his mind. "If I go, who's gonna take care of Pari?"

"I wanna go!" Pari exclaimed, right on cue. "Please, Jason, let me go with you! I've always wanted to see their home! Please, Jason? Please?"

Jason was about to say something, but he reluctantly glanced at the fairy. "Your call."

"I will take care of her while you are making arrangements with your father," the fairy replied, a grin beginning to form on her face. "I will protect her with my life. I see how much she means to you."

"So I can go? Thank you, thank you, thank you, thank you!" Pari exclaimed, before tightly hugging the fairy's leg.

The fairy chuckled uncomfortably as she shook the little girl off. She then proceeded to lead Jason and Pari to the forest, where hopefully all his questions would be answered.

*

"I barely remember this place." Jason was still trying to process the situation as anything but a weird dream, but he could hardly think with Pari's overenthusiastic chittering beside him. She was going on about how she had always wanted to see the fairies, and which ones in particular she was going to visit, and which ones were her friends, and which ones she wanted to avoid, and what she was going to do while she was there and so on, *ad nauseam.*

"Most of your memory of this place was erased a long time ago," the fairy explained. "Somehow, though, you still kept coming back. Please, be quiet!" she interrupted herself, turning to Pari, who shut up immediately. "I had wanted to interpret that as curiosity, as a desire to find something the humans said wasn't there. I had wanted to know that it was your heart that was leading you back to me."

"Heart. Yeah, something like that."

The fairy chuckled. "I'm not upset. What did you say? You, ah, moved on."

"Yeah."

"Oh, in all that excitement," the fairy added, "I forgot to introduce myself properly. My name is Ortho. I am a messenger. I figured, after a while, you would want to stop calling me the 'Shiny Lady.' You ... are an adult now, after all."

"Ortho. That's a ... a different name."

"Well, I could say the same about yours, *Jason*," Ortho retorted, before adding, "I know all of this is still very strange to you, and should you choose to stay, it'll take a while for you to adjust. After you meet the soldiers, though, everything will start to make more sense."

As they walked through the forest, their path became illuminated with scattered will-o-wisps and what looked like large fireflies. Pari was ecstatic; Jason was confused.

"Are these the, uh, the soldiers?"

Ortho chuckled nervously and shook her head. "Goodness, no. You underestimate Gregōr. He would never let the sprites be a part of his army. They are too weak, he says. Like bugs."

Jason frowned. "Gregōr? Who's that?"

"He is the ruler of our land," Ortho replied. "He only allows the strongest and the purest to be in his very presence, let alone his army. Those he only turns away are the, uh, the lucky ones."

Jason did not want to know what that meant. "Sounds like a nice guy."

Ortho whispered in Jason's ear. "He and his soldiers are not what the humans would imagine the Fae to be. They are not what they would *want* to imagine the Fae to be. Gregōr is nothing less

questionMark 29

than a tyrant, a murderer. I would rather not have Pari meet him. It is ... It is for your own good." She spoke up again. "No one has complained about him and his leadership. Our territory has been ... well protected for the past two hundred years because of him."

"He must be really powerful," Pari observed.

"Yes," Ortho replied. "He ... He is."

Soon, they were standing in front of the entrance to a large, underground cavern barely lit by a path of pulsating wisps and flickering lanterns.

"This is where Gregōr lives," Ortho said. "He is expecting you. I will take Pari to my home where she will be safe. The messengers and sprites will protect her while I wait for you to return."

"Wait," Jason said, "you mean Gregōr, the—" When Ortho hushed him, Jason immediately got the message. "The ... ruler of your land, he wants to see me?"

"Yes," Ortho replied hurriedly, "he has heard all about you. He will ... he will help to teach you the ways of our people, and after that, you will be ... reunited with your father. Now, go! He does not like to be kept waiting. He probably already knows you're here."

Startled, Jason made his way down into the cavern, not knowing what to expect from the "ruler of their land" Gregōr. He followed the flickering path farther and farther away from the moonlight of the surface world.

There were not flames inside the hanging lanterns, Jason discovered when he decided to stop and look closely at one of them. Instead, there were tiny sprites like the ones he had seen outside, furiously and desperately flickering as they struggled to escape their glass prisons. There were usually five or six in each lantern; however, in the dimmer lanterns, only three or four (sometimes, even fewer) were still buzzing around, still trying fruitlessly to escape. The rest were dead; limp, humanlike corpses each barely the size of his index finger lay in a heap at the bottom of each lantern. Jason had even witnessed one of the sprites flicker out and die: the poor creature had used every ounce of its remaining energy in a futile attempt to break the glass wall, but its firefly-like glow had extinguished for good, and the sprite's corpse slid limply down the side of the wall to the edge of the pile, where it lay unmoving.

Jason managed to tear his eyes away from the lantern. What did he care? What happened to them was none of his business ... but the fact that Gregōr seemed to have captured them just for the sake of using them as light sources, and then leaving them to die ... No, they were just bug-like things, like fireflies. Really big fireflies. Human-shaped fireflies. Kids did this stuff to fireflies all the time. It was really nothing to worry about.

If they look like bugs, a voice inside his head told him, *they should be treated like bugs.*

Then again ...

A few will-o-wisps met him and guided him the rest of the way through the labyrinth, although they didn't make the journey any less ominous. Eventually, the wisps dispersed into a colossal chamber, the heart of the cave. Jason saw a swarm of them hypnotically hover above a massive lake, giving the illusion that its surface sparkled and reflected the moon and stars that weren't there.

The wisps illuminated the entire chamber, although it couldn't offset the sense of foreboding that had stayed with him throughout his whole journey. On the lake were two rows of islands and a long bridge that cut between them, an aisle. The islands closest to him were only small hills, but as the aisle stretched farther away, the islands began to turn into mountains themselves, although none of them could compare to their Everest at the heart of the lake, where Jason assumed Gregōr lived.

On each island stood a man about as tall as Ortho wearing thick brown armor with black padding. These men must have been the soldiers Ortho was talking about. They were nothing like he had imagined them to be. They weren't ... *fairies*. They didn't even have wings. Then again, neither did Ortho at first, but it was clear that these guys didn't tote around friggin' tutus and magic wands.

Before Jason could get a good look at anything else, the swing of a sword and the roaring pain in his arm caused him to cry out and fall against one of the smaller islands. It was then that he noticed what the "islands" were actually made of: Jason's body was forced against a prickly pile of bones that dug into his back like cacti. He saw a golden glimmer out of the corner of his eye and, hoping for a distraction from the pain in both his back and his arm (which he knew was bleeding—*bad*), turned his head to look at it. There was a pair of brown-booted feet directly in front of his face.

Startled, Jason turned his head again and immediately noticed the tip of a sword pointed at the base of his neck. It belonged to one of the soldiers, presumably the one who had attacked him in the first place, who loomed over him with a stoic brown-and-black-painted face and a vengeful fire in his eyes.

"What is your business here, human?" the soldier above him asked, the sword at Jason's neck hardly wavering.

Jason was too petrified to respond.

"How did you find this place?" the second soldier clarified, the booted feet by Jason's face hardly shifting as he also unsheathed his weapon and pointed it at the base of Jason's neck. When Jason looked up at him, he looked nearly identical to the first soldier. "Speak, and you will have ample time to prepare your last words."

It was then that Jason found his voice. "Gregōr! I'm here to see Gregōr. Ortho sent me. She says that Gregōr ... Gregōr can help me find my father. Apparently, I'm ... she says I'm a changeling or something. My ... My name is Jason, uh ... Jason Vega, or ... or I don't know what you would call me, what ... what name you would have for me, what, uh, what name I'd be under."

Now, it was the soldiers' turn to be petrified. In one swift movement, they both lowered their weapons and turned to each other, quietly discussing something. Jason took the opportunity to shuffle to his feet, knocking some of the bones into the shallower part of the lake. His back ached, and his now completely red forearm stung horribly. He just wanted some freakin' answers.

Finally, the soldiers turned back to Jason.

"My apologies. We didn't recognize you. This way," the first soldier replied, before walking stiffly to the bridge and toward the mountain in the center of the lake.

Jason could barely process the soldier's comment. They didn't recognize him? What did that mean? Whoever he was supposed to be here, was he really important enough to have to be *recognized* by the soldiers? There was only one way to find out. The second soldier stayed behind on his island and glanced curiously at Jason as he dizzily sloshed through the shallow water and caught up to his guide.

All of the islands were made of bones and gold shards, Jason realized. Even the mountain in the center of the lake, their destination. But where did Gregōr get all those bones and all that gold? His stomach sank as he thought of an answer to the former question, thinking back to the sprites in the lanterns.

As they ascended the mountain, Jason tried to keep his balance so he wouldn't fall onto the bones again. They crunched beneath Jason's and his guide's feet, and some even slid down to the mountain's base, but Jason managed to keep a good foothold for the most part until they were close enough to see its sole occupant: Gregōr, the feared leader of the fairies (that, Jason admitted, was a ... strange combination of words).

Gregōr made the other soldiers look like sprites in comparison. He was at least eight feet tall and built like a lion: a giant frame, lean and protruding muscles, and a predator's eyes that would haunt Jason for the rest of his life. He had the same brown and black armor as the rest of his soldiers, but Gregōr's armor had an additional layer made of bones, most likely those of his once-enemies. There was a human skull propped snugly on each shoulder and ribcages of various sizes hugging his arms and legs. His breastplate was mostly composed of large leg and thigh bones threaded together; nothing else, Jason realized, would have been formidable enough to support and protect the gargantuan man.

"Gregōr," Jason's guide spoke up, bowing his head at his ruler's name. "This human wishes to speak with you. He was brought by Ortho. He says he is Zelimyr."

At this, Gregōr raised an eyebrow, and his gaze became more sympathetic, although not by much.

"Brought?" Gregōr had a thick, intimidating accent. Was it German? Russian? Schwarzenegger? Jason couldn't place it. Still, it was so thick that Jason could hardly make out the tyrant's words. "From where?"

The soldier glanced at Jason, who took this as a cue to speak.

"Ortho, she ... she came to my home, and she told me the truth ... Sir. She told me you would be able to help me find my father."

"Your father," Gregōr repeated, chuckling to himself. After a moment, he added to the soldier, "Go, and reward Ortho! She will feast well tonight."

The soldier bowed to Gregōr, before turning around and walking partway down the mountain. However, instead of walking the rest of the way, he stopped, before a huge gust of wind erupted from the ground beneath him, similar to what had happened when Ortho had first revealed herself. However, the wings that burst from the soldier's back were not Ortho's graceful, hypnotic wings. Instead, these were massive beetle-like wings that pounded at the rate of a jet engine as the soldier crouched low, preparing to take flight. He leaped into the air and shot through the cavern tunnels like a heat-seeking missile as the buzzing of his wings faded into the darkness.

Jason had been knocked off his feet, but this time, he had caught himself before the massive pile of bones could impale him again and possibly drag him down the mountain. Once he caught his breath, Jason muttered, "Damn, that was cool."

"I suppose," Gregōr commented, having heard him, "it is impressive for someone who has never seen *real* Fae before."

Jason shakily stood up and faced Gregōr.

"'*Real* Fae'?" he asked. "So are you a—?" Jason stopped himself.

As if reading his mind, Gregōr narrowed his eyes and asked, "A *what*?"

"You know, um ... uh ... what did you say, um ... a Fae?"

Gregōr frowned, and the distaste slowly spread across his face until he had the scowl and curled upper lip of a demonic bear.

"I knew what you were about to say," he rumbled, each word rising up from the deepest, darkest pits of Hell. "I've heard the human term, and that's likely the one you've heard, too. It's derogatory, a slur, don't you think, now that you've seen what the forest-dwellers, the Fae really are? From now on, you will not say that word in my presence, or there will be grave consequences. Unless, of course," Gregōr added, his tone noticeably lightening, "you are using it to refer to the sprites and messengers."

"Yeah, um ... t-that's what it mostly refers to, yes. That word. They, uh, the title—the word was more meant for them. Meant for creatures *like* them. Their, uh, their lack of strength and power. That is what t-that word is describing." Part of him still wasn't fully convinced that this was real, that he was just on some crazy LSD trip, but the only choice he had at the moment was to go with the flow. To hope he wouldn't screw up and make Gregōr kill him on the spot.

"The fact that you agree," a jubilant smile spread across Gregōr's face where hellish anger had been only moments earlier, "only further proves that you are your father's child."

"Great," Jason replied, trying to decide whether Gregōr's jovial mood was less or more unsettling. "So, speaking of my dad, uh, where is he? Is he, uh, one of the soldiers or something?"

Suddenly, Gregōr let out a booming laugh that nearly made half the islands crumble. Some of the wisps fled, but the soldiers standing on the islands were unfazed, bound to their duties.

"Dim-witted wench!" Gregōr exclaimed, roaring with laughter. "Ortho knows full well who your father is, and she refused to say a thing! I will forgive her, though, because Zelimyr has come home at last."

"... Eh?"

Gregōr cackled, wrapping a thick, muscular arm around Jason's body and holding him close to his side. He now understood what it felt like to be a paranoid kid's teddy bear. "Do I have to do everything? Zelimyr, you are not the son of one of my soldiers. You are the son of *mine*. You are of *my* blood, and the fact that you see the sprites and messengers as inferior creatures only proves it more."

"O-Okay," Jason gasped, still trying to process everything that had just happened. Things had just surpassed drug trip level of weird. "I'm ... lost. You're ... *You're* my father?"

"Yes," Gregōr replied, releasing Jason so air could reach his lungs again. "You see, many years ago, you were taken from me and sent to live with those *animals* you call humans. Not only that, but you missed your coming-of-age. I had tracked you down, pinpointed your location so that we could bring you home, but you were missing." At this, he narrowed his eyes. Yes, that was *definitely* vengeance. "I was afraid I had lost you forever. But, now, you are home, and you will stay with us instead of going back to those animals, yes? You will take back your kingdom and your people?" Before Jason had a chance to respond, Gregōr continued, "I thought so, my boy. It must have been as much a smear on your honor as it had been on mine. I can't imagine what it must have been like. Thinking about it sickens me. But rest assured, my son. I will find whoever was responsible for your disappearance, and they will pay ... dearly."

Gregōr noticed the bleeding wound on Jason's arm.

"You're hurt," the tyrant observed. "I know this is from one of my soldiers. I should not blame them, though, and neither should you. He was doing his duty, and for him to have thought you were a trespasser, he was doing it well. As my heir, you will soon understand this better. However, for now, you must be healed. Go back to Ortho, rest for the night, and return to me in the morning. Then, I will teach you our ways."

*

When Jason left the cavern, Ortho found him and guided him back to her home, which Jason immediately recognized as the Shiny Lady's glade. There, they found Pari playing with some of the sprites. Seeing the sprites now, free and buzzing happily around his sister, Jason could hardly comprehend that these were the same creatures Gregōr had used as his unwilling lanterns, the same creatures that he had seen lay dead in heaps at the bottoms of their glass prisons ...

Pari jumped to her feet and ran toward Jason and Ortho.

"Jason! You're back! How was it? Did you get to meet Gregōr? Did you get to meet your dad? Was he nice? How were they?"

"My father was—" Jason started, before remembering Ortho's request from earlier. "...Nice. You might even get to meet him, but not for a while. He's ... busy."

"Okay, Jason," Pari said. "Now, I'd like you to meet some of my friends."

"Alright," Jason replied, although he was more focused on the stinging pain of his arm, which Ortho was in the process of healing. The bloody gash, he noticed, went straight through one of his old tattoos, a bright red heart with the name "Lily" etched into it. Lily had been one of his high school girlfriends, Jason reflected. They had broken up when they discovered they were going to separate colleges. The reality of his situation began to sink in a little more.

Pari went to talk to some of the sprites who were still there, and she pointed at Jason. As soon as they got a glimpse of him, they scattered like a flock of birds shaken from a tree.

"Hey! Hey, where'd you go? Come back, he won't hurt you. He's nice!"

While Pari chased after them, Ortho whispered, "Was he kind, really?"

"In a way, yeah. I mean, he was understanding. Kind of."

"As understanding as he can be," Ortho murmured, still tending to Jason's wound.

"I guess."

"He didn't scare you too much, did he?"

"Nah," Jason said, wincing a little at the pain. "Nah, I'll ... I'll get used to it."

"It's better you don't," Ortho replied. "It's better you stay at least a little scared of him. It feeds his ego more. I learned that the hard way."

"Ah. I won't ask if, you know, you don't want to talk about it. I mean ... Now, I understand why everyone's so terrified of this guy. But ... Ortho?"

"Yes, Jason?"

"... I don't know if I can do this. I mean, it would have been fine if my dad was a ... an accountant or ... a tooth fairy, or whatever the hell kind of jobs you have here. I would've actually loved it if he was like you and had all those ... X-Men powers and stuff. But ... *him*? Gregōr? If you're saying I have to be scared of this guy for the rest of my life ... I don't know if I can live like that."

Ortho nodded, looking a little forlorn. "I understand. Do you want to go back?"

"That's the thing," Jason replied, "I don't know if he'll *let* me. What would he say if I turned him down? What would he *do*? If what you're telling me is true, and if the kind of shit I saw in there is any indication, I don't think he'd be very happy. 'Cause it looks like no one has said 'no' to him and *lived*. So part of me really does want to go home with Pari—it's been fun, see ya later, *sayonara*, good-*freakin'*-bye—and forget all this happened. But at the same time, Gregōr looks like the kind of guy who's gonna hunt me down and kidnap me or even kill me if I don't do what he says. So, which is it? Can I go home safely and 'never see or hear from you again,' or do I have to look over my shoulder every day for the rest of my life in fear of my *psychotic dad*?"

Ortho paused for a moment, taking all this in while Jason panted, exhausted from his outburst. She closed her eyes and sighed. "You're right. I lied to you."

Jason's eyes widened. "As in, *deliberately* lied? You wanted me to meet him *that* bad?"

"I wanted to end his rampage. I wanted to protect you. If he knew you had returned to your human home, he would have taken you himself, forcing you through the ceremony and … I don't know what would happen then. He would probably force you to become a monster like him or keep you prisoner in his cave. It would have been better to make it look like we had brought you back, or you had come back on your own, so long as you appeared willing to return."

"The prodigal son," Jason muttered in reply, but Ortho ignored him.

"I'm sorry I had to lie to you like that, but I had to say what I could in order to convince you to return. It was for your own safety. I promise I won't lie to you again, Jason."

Before Ortho could continue, Pari returned.

"I guess they still don't like you for some reason," she said to Jason, sitting down at Ortho's feet. "Maybe it's because you act like a jerk sometimes, and they only like nice people."

"Yeah, I … I guess that's it."

*

The next morning, Jason intended to meet Gregōr at the fortress, but to his surprise, Gregōr was already outside waiting for him.

Damn, Jason thought. *He must be really happy to have me back.*

He tried to keep his breathing even as he approached his father, remembering his conversation with Ortho before he and Pari had gone to sleep. Stay a little afraid of him, but look like you really want to be there. Just like college. Just like—

Shit.

"Zelimyr! My boy! It's about time you came. You rested well?"

"Yes, Dad. Father. Er, whatever you want me to call you."

"'Father' is fine," Gregōr replied. "Or you may call me 'Gregōr,' as everyone else does. Whatever makes you comfortable, my boy. Now, I will show you our land and way of life. Come! The day is only so long."

Everywhere they went, Jason noticed that the nearby Fae scattered as soon as he and Gregōr were within sight. The sprites and pixies seemed to vanish into thin air, and the messengers climbed the thick trees, hid behind bushes and retreated into caves. However, Jason did notice one other thing that had slipped under Gregōr's radar: the Fae, especially the messengers, always fled with a brief look of disgust ... and disappointment.

"Do your kind interact with humans often?" The question had been on Jason's mind for a while, but he had wanted to wait until Gregōr was in a better mood to ask, which had been a wise move on his part.

"Not mine. Not ours, my boy," Gregōr replied, and despite being jubilant, his tone was surprisingly restrained. "The sprites and messengers, they do. They are the ones who always show themselves to them. They are friendly to them. Entertain them. Love them, even. Enjoy companionship. Especially the offspring, ah, what do the humans call them?"

"Children?"

"Yes, thank you, 'children.' I suppose you would be the one to know, wouldn't you?" Gregōr asked, before roaring with laughter. "But, yes, for some reason, the sprites and messengers find the

questionMark

children entertaining."

"And, uh, you don't?" As soon as those words came out of his mouth, Jason wished he could shove them back in.

"Of course not!" Gregōr boomed, although he was thankfully (*thankfully*) still in good spirits (*thankfully*). "I hear they are awful, worse than the adults in terms of territory boundaries and just general intolerance. Humanlings, children, whatever you call them, they chitter too much, as well. Chitter, chitter, chitter. Worse than birds and squirrels and chipmunks. Speaking of which," he interrupted himself, "I've been hearing reports from scouts saying that they've been hearing a lot of that chittering lately, around here especially." He narrowed his eyes in Jason's direction. "More than usual, I might add. Would you know anything about it?"

Jason's stomach fell. He had forgotten to remind Pari to be quiet or to warn her about the soldiers. He had been so absorbed in his own dilemma ...

"I usually have my soldiers go and take care of them if I ever find them trespassing here," Gregōr continued when Jason didn't respond. "Well, if my *soldiers* ever find them trespassing. I never see them personally."

Jason froze. "You've never seen one?"

"No!" Gregōr replied, stopping as well and looking over his shoulder at his son. "Why would I need to? I have no business with them, but I still respect the fact that they are ... useful to us."

Jason was afraid to ask what his father had meant by that.

*

"Whatcha eatin', Miss Ortho?"

Ortho tore her eyes away from the "reward" she had earned from Gregōr. She didn't want to eat the large slab of meat when Pari was around, but the little girl had managed to sneak up on her. Startled, the messenger replied, "Deer. Gregōr was so happy that ... that Jason and his father are back together now, that one of his soldiers got ... deer meat."

"Okay." This answer seemed to satisfy Pari for now. "Can I

try some?"

"You wouldn't like it."

"I've had it before. A long time ago, but I've had it."

"You wouldn't like this kind."

Pari shrugged. "If you say so. Bye, Miss Ortho!"

Pari ran back to the sprites she had been playing with earlier, leaving Ortho to reflect on the events of the previous night. Had it been worth ending their people's pain, at least for now? Had it been a good idea in the first place? The last thing Ortho wanted was for more innocent lives to be lost because of Gregōr's quarter-century rage, but she still wasn't sure he deserved the reunion. From what Jason had told her, it had been a happy one, even though he had gotten dangerously hurt by one of the soldiers. But there was still the issue of what Gregōr *did* deserve. Twenty-five years was brief compared to some of Gregōr's other fits of rage, but this by far had been his worst. She knew his pain, but at the same time, she couldn't shake the fact that Zelimyr's reappearance was much too generous a gift for someone like Gregōr …

*

"So, you like your new home?" Gregōr asked, grinning as they ate some meat the soldiers had caught for them.

Fake an answer. That was all Jason could do at this point. Fake it till you make it. "Yeah. I mean, I think I could get used to it."

"Good! Good!" Gregōr's jovial mood returned. "You are my son, after all. And the best part? I will train you as one of my soldiers. You will be the most powerful of them all. You will be my second. How do you feel about that, Zelimyr?"

"To be honest …" To be honest? It scared him. He thought about what would happen if he turned back at this point, took Pari, said goodbye to Ortho and headed home. If Gregōr knew where he lived—and, like Ortho said, he somehow found out Jason still lived there—then he and Pari weren't safe. They'd probably have to move upstate or at least stay with someone else for a while until Gregōr gave up looking. When would that be? Also, how would he explain the situation to any of his friends he wanted to move in with? Not only would he have to explain why his sister was with him, but there was also the matter of being on the run from mythical creatures trying to kill them both. Even his stoner friends would have thought he was nuts at that point. He was cornered. " ... I'm kind of ... excited. I mean, I've always dreamed about stuff like this," he continued, trying to convince himself as well as Gregōr. "Y'know, kick ass for a living and stuff. Fight ... bears. I mean, this wasn't the way I *expected* to, y'know, live how I want, but ... it's here, I like it, it's cool. It's cool. Uh, when did you say the ceremony was?"

"It can be whenever you like. Tomorrow, if you wish," Gregōr replied, laughing. Thankfully, he was falling for it.

"Alright, I can deal with that." Tomorrow was his birthday, Jason remembered. He supposed there was irony in it somewhere, but there were more important things on his mind at the moment. "And, well, what about my, uh ... well, my life with ...?"

"Oh, simple," Gregōr replied. "You fake your death. Nothing complicated."

"Fake my death?" Jason grimaced. Gregōr's reply had been a little too casual for his liking.

"Cover your human garments with blood and leave them somewhere. A classic technique. Someone's bound to find them eventually."

"No, uh ... No magic?"

Gregōr cackled as he usually did when Jason asked questions like this. "Magic? You have much to learn, my boy. That is all the sprites' and messengers' doing. We don't need those silly tricks."

Jason was about to mention that, yeah, they might come in handy, but he wisely kept his mouth shut. There was no arguing with Gregōr, especially now.

*

Jason had returned to Ortho stripped to his black boxers. He lay on the ground, his entire upper body of tattoos now exposed to the wilderness. Ortho examined the body art quizzically; elaborate murals on his chest and back, with snakes and dragons running up and down his arms, dotted with signatures and other small images, including the heart tattoo where the gash had now scabbed over.

"What did Gregōr say when he saw that?" she asked him, a hint of amusement in her voice.

"Just what you'd expect. I look like a warrior, and my ink's gonna look really good with my armor." He groaned as he stood up. "Where's Pari?"

"Hiding," Ortho replied quietly. "Some of the soldiers were passing through earlier. I wanted to make sure she was out of sight in case they wanted to stop and talk. Some of the sprites are looking after her."

Jason nodded. "Good. I don't know how long we can keep doing this, though. I mean, if I could let her stay, I would. She doesn't have anywhere else to go." He sighed, leaning against a tree and grimacing as the bark rubbed up against his bare back. "Let's face it, if there *was* anywhere else for her to go, she would have been put there by now."

"'Been' put?" Ortho asked, approaching him. "So she would have been taken, as you thought I had tried to do."

"Yeah. I know I'm not the most responsible guy in the world, but I at least want to take care of her, you know? I wanted her to grow up with someone she actually knew, like family, instead of, y'know, in a foster home. I've had some friends who have been through there, and … yeah, it sucks." He scratched his head, feeling some ticks.

"Mm-hmm."

"And I know I haven't been the best brother to her, much less the best dad, but … I tried, you know? I'm still trying." He tried to pry the ticks off his scalp, and the near-futile effort helped get his mind off the situation for the time being.

They were both silent for a long time, the stillness broken only by some bushes rustling nearby. Ortho tensed, but she relaxed when she saw Pari's head poke out from her hiding place.

"Jason! You're back!" She squeezed out of her small cavern. "What'd they do to your clothes?"

"That's not important right now," Jason replied, approaching her and kneeling down so he could look her in the eye. Her clothes were all dirty from spending so much time out in the forest (and she probably had ticks as well, although they didn't seem to bother her as much), but she was still as happy as could be. She wrapped him in a tight hug and a chill ran down his spine. "Pari, I ... I'm going to stay. I told ... my dad that I'm going to stay here."

"So you're going to be one of the fairies?" Pari asked, before whispering, "Are you going to learn magic?"

Jason chuckled, although it was flat with disappointment. "Yeah, I asked him about that. My dad. He said, uh ... He said no. But, trust me, if there's any way I could, I would, especially the stuff Ortho can do." He looked up at her, smirking.

Ortho chuckled. "I don't know if he would approve of that."

"Still, I don't think he realizes how *useful* magic would be in fighting. I could name all kinds of really, really powerful people who have magic or ... something like it."

"Humans?" Ortho raised an eyebrow.

"Well, fictional humans. Humans in, uh, lore or whatever you call it ... I'll explain it someday."

"So can I live here with you?" Pari asked.

Everyone was silent for a long time, the joy of the moment having been sucked out by that one question. Jason finally spoke up.

"Well, that's the thing. You can't."

"What do you mean?"

"Pari ..." he glanced over at Ortho, his eyes pleading for her assistance. However, she did nothing. "It's not safe for you here."

"But ... you'll protect me, won't you, Miss Ortho?" Pari asked, running over to the taller woman.

"Not forever," Ortho admitted. "They'd eventually find you."

"'They'? Who's 'they'?" She turned back toward Jason.

"Gregōr," he explained. "Gregōr and the soldiers, they ... they don't like humans here. My, uh, my dad wanted to let you stay, but Gregōr got mad at him. He tried his best, but it, uh ... it looks like it's just gonna be me here."

"Well, what am I gonna do without you?" Pari asked, returning to Jason.

The words were painful to pull up from his throat. He set his hands on her shoulders. "Pari, I want you to ... to leave. As soon as possible. Go to the police. Tell them I'm dead. They'll find somewhere safe for you to go."

"But … I'm never gonna see you again."

"It's for the best," Ortho added, and Pari turned to her in disbelief before turning back to Jason.

"I want you to know that I love you more than anything else, and I just want you to be safe," Jason continued. "I … I always want the best for you, and like I told Ortho earlier, I'm sorry I've never been able to give it. But this is what's gotta happen now, and you gotta promise to leave, okay? Remember what I said the other night about keeping promises? You need to …" There was a lump in his throat that he struggled to fight back. "You need to keep your promises—if you say you're gonna do something, you gotta do it, okay? You gotta leave. You gotta remember … not to come back."

Pari's eyes were welling up. "Yeah. I promise. I love you, Jason."

"I love you, too, Pari. But you gotta leave now. Gregor's preoccupied since the ceremony's tomorrow, so you'll have plenty of time to get back to the house. Get what you need. Okay? Then go straight to the police."

"Okay."

They embraced for the last time, Jason holding his sister tight and still whispering in her ear.

"Now," he said when they let go, his voice breaking, "I'm going to close my eyes and count to ten. By the time I'm done … you better be gone. You better be far away from here."

"You promise you'll be alright?" Pari asked.

"I promise." After a few more moments of looking into her eyes, Jason whispered, "Bye, Pari," closed his eyes, and began to count.

*

"You're worried about her, aren't you?"

"Yeah. I just … I hope she's alright."

"She's a smart girl. She'll follow through."

"I hope so."

The next morning, Ortho was helping Jason prepare for the coming-of-age ceremony. The armor he had to wear felt incredibly big on him (although that was mainly because Jason was about a foot shorter and much scrawnier than most of the soldiers), and that godforsaken paint Ortho had put on his face was itchy and uncomfortable (what was this shit made of, poison ivy?).

"So I wanted to get this out of the way before the whole ... coming-of-age thing happens."

"Yes, Jason?"

"What happened? When I was born, I mean. I keep hearing Gregōr's side, but I have a good feeling that's not the whole story." He turned his head a little, glancing at her over his shoulder. "I mean, no offense, but I'm still kind of pissed that you flat out lied to me about having to stay here, so the least you can do is, you know, tell me the truth now that I've agreed to stay."

Ortho sighed and started to fix Jason's hair, forcing him to face forward again. "Yes. I supposed you'd ask that sooner or later. Gregōr has been asking this question for many years now, and ... innocent lives have been lost because he didn't know the answer. No one else here knows except for me and some of the other messengers, so when I tell you this, you must promise never to tell anyone, especially Gregōr or anyone directly associated with him."

"I promise."

"Okay," Ortho sighed, before whispering, "You were not supposed to have been given to the humans as a changeling. That was, as you could imagine, Gregōr's worst nightmare, so he protected you with twice the diligence and fervor he put toward the fortress itself. He had a grand plan in mind for his son, and, by God, he was going to follow through with it. I remember. He always said that Zelimyr would grow up to be his finest apprentice, and he would become the finest warrior the Fae had ever known. He would have given everything to make sure that his only son would grow up to be a strong, brave ruler like him. Everything, as far as Gregōr was concerned, was going perfectly. One day, however, through an elaborate plan by the messengers, you were stolen and replaced with a human infant in the rare moment Gregōr and his soldiers had been distracted. This is the story Gregōr knows. From that day on, his reign had become unbearable due to his inconsolable rage, which only became worse as time went on. He searched the forest for you day and night, and he swore vengeance on whoever had dared to capture or even kill his only son." Ortho lowered her voice further, almost mouthing her next confession. "He never found out that I was the one who took you and gave you to your human family."

"Why?" Jason asked, his voice equally low. "What made you think that I would be better off with them?"

"Because Gregōr deserved it. I and the other messengers felt as though he needed a comeuppance of some kind, something he would see as a smear to his honor. And I also felt that, at the same time, he needed an opportunity to see that humans weren't the vermin he imagined them to be, that they had value. The plan had worked well at first, but ... we had not expected him to discover the fraud child so soon."

"He said he had never seen a human child in his life."

Ortho bowed her head. "It did not live long enough to become a child."

"You mean ...?" Jason's stomach turned. His whole life had not only been a lie, but it had been *stolen* from someone else. The real Jason was supposed to be in college trying to find a job, staying afloat and helping take care of his family. But the real Jason never had a chance to go to college. He never even had a chance to go to school. Never had the chance to make any friends, never had the chance to play ... most likely, he never had the chance to even walk or talk. Jason—the fake Jason—had stolen all of that from him. He felt sick. "Oh, my God."

"He had murdered many others over the course of your life, but one instance was, well ... especially tragic. Your coming-of-age—your original coming-of-age—was growing near, and he had made another attempt to search for you—or, at least, he had made another attempt to torture unfortunate prisoners for information. Finally, a sprite had revealed your human family's location, and he and his soldiers went to find you. However, you weren't there."

"When was that?"

"Seven years ago."

Jason paled.

"And ... what did they do to the people who were?"

"But, you see, some good has come out of this. I-If Gregōr would not see the value of humans, then you certainly would. And you do, because of your ... concern."

"Yeah, but what happened to them? What happened to my family?"

"Your human family," Ortho hastily corrected. She was grimacing, trying hard not to cry. "And ... I'd rather not say. I don't know the full details, and I'd rather you not ask Gregōr about it. Besides, it's ... it's in the past. It's all in the past. It's ... it's in the past."

"Ortho, what happened to them? Tell me what happened to them!"

"There's nothing we can do about it. Now, come on. Don't be like that." She stood him up and began to lead him away from the glade toward the fortress.

"*What did he do to them?*" He struggled against her, but her grip on his arms was firm.

"Please don't be like that. The ceremony's about to start. Please, don't make it wait any more than it has."

"Ortho!"

"Please, don't make it wait ..."

*

The newly christened Zelimyr sat with his father at the peak of their mountain. Gregōr's cavern was a dreary place, but Zelimyr knew he would get used to living and training here eventually.

The ceremony had gone according to plan. Zelimyr didn't fully understand what was going on—something about a "blood awakening", something had been injected into his veins, and the process of growing the wings had been one of the most painful things in his life. Still, it had been done. Seven years late, but, as the humans say, there was no time like the present.

Gregōr had taken some time after the ceremony to teach him how to fly. Tomorrow, Gregōr had said, would be fully devoted to continuing those lessons, starting with teaching Zelimyr how to control himself during flight: how to turn, how to stop, and how to not crash into trees.

However, there was no time to worry about that now. Now was the time to celebrate the christening with special meat that Gregōr had harvested and prepared himself. It was a Fae tradition, Gregōr had said, reserved only for very special occasions.

"This is actually really good," Zelimyr said in between bites of a limb. "You never told me exactly what this was."

Gregōr chuckled in between bites of his own hearty meal. "I told you, it's a rare treat."

There were more piles of gold and bones at the bottom of the lake, underwater mountains that weren't quite tall enough to break the surface and become islands. Unbeknownst to Zelimyr, though, at the top of one of these mountains was an item that was neither gold nor bone, but a single pink, sparkly Converse shoe.

Food

*H*e had hanged himself in the pantry of his own soup kitchen, surrounded by rotten food.

Those who had discovered him were shocked—at the event itself, at the identity of the dead man, and most of all at the brief suicide note they had found on one of the sludge-covered shelves. This man had been very generous in his life, a shining example for humanitarians. Only something incredibly drastic would have caused him to take his own life, but what? What had led him to leave this earth and begin his final words with, "I know I have dealt with …"?

*

… the Devil.

Marion looked the dark figure in the eye. He told himself he was prepared to resist any sort of temptation the unholy creature would offer him, but in reality, he was desperate, helpless. Long strings of prayers coursed through his mind at unfathomable speed, and God himself could almost hear the agony of Marion's immortal soul. What man had ever found himself face to face with the Devil, or any other specter capable of his dark sorcery? Who or what could have possibly prepared him for an encounter like this, where the Serpent had chosen to manifest to him alone? Why had he been chosen to be tempted, to have his divine faith tested by a deceptively simple choice?

The Devil was waiting. It felt like an eternity had passed since he had asked the question, and Marion was still trying to compose an answer. Marion's gaze shifted to the ground, not wanting to look into those serpentine eyes and let their influence poison his thoughts.

He had two options: the first was to resist, to call upon God to protect him from the dark one's temptations, to drive the creature back to Hell and let him wait for another unfortunate soul to seduce. With the small Crucifix around his neck, he could do it. He just needed the resolve to keep the darkness out of his mind and heart.

But the second option had come to him in a sudden burst of inspiration: this was a chance, Marion realized, to *trick* the Devil, to destroy him with his own power. He would need to beat the Devil at his own game, deceive *him* into thinking he had won. If he made this choice, though, he would need to think carefully about what he said, to phrase his answer in a way that allowed no loopholes, no possible deviations that the Devil could exploit. It would be difficult, but Marion believed it was possible.

"One wish? And no price?"

"No price now, but you will pay in time."

Marion's stomach turned; the nausea induced by the Devil's reply threatened to spread through the rest of his body, but he couldn't afford to show any sign of fear. Fear was what the Devil fed upon, what made him grow stronger and his influence more constricting. Instead, the mortal man stood his ground and looked back up at the specter, looked him in his fiery eyes. From whom Marion could only guess was God, a rush of bravery began to course through him.

"And what if I refuse? What if I want nothing?" He caught himself reaching up and holding onto the Crucifix as if for his life. The stream of prayers for divine strength continued as he anticipated the Devil's response.

"Then you are lying," the Devil replied nonchalantly, although his expression didn't change. "If you say you wish for nothing, then you will continue to have nothing. Nothing changes; you will remain poor, and grow poorer by the day. You would have lost your opportunity to have anything of this world, anything at all, with no foul consequence."

"No foul consequence." The Devil could sense the skepticism in Marion's voice.

"You may think I destroy," he explained with a bemused twinkle in his eyes, "but I also have the power to create, as I would do for you if you chose to accept my offer." He scrutinized Marion, taking note of every minute movement of the mortal man's face. A wry, wiry smile stretched across his own, the corners of his mouth curling around the tips of his pointed ears. "You don't trust me."

"Why should I? I know you."

"And I know you, the God-fearing man," the Devil retorted, still in his calm, dismissive monotone. "You say you don't need any of what I'm offering, no wealth or titles. After all, no earthly possessions could amount to what God in Heaven has in store when all is said and done." His smile waned a little, but not enough to be noticeable. "Personally, I don't believe that, but I respect it far more than you could ever understand. I can't help but ask, though: is it enough?"

"It is far more than you could ever give me."

The smile vanished completely, and suddenly, it was clear that, indeed, this *was* the Devil himself. His icy glare pierced every inch of Marion's mortal flesh, singed him with spears of magma, and it seemed to last an eternity. A small flicker of relief came every time the monster blinked, but the burst of pain would soon begin again, each iteration overpowering the last. Marion couldn't help but wonder how long his newfound bravery would last against this torture, when it would finally abandon him to the whims of the specter.

"More than I could give you!" the Devil hissed, spitting out every word and biting its tail end. With every word, the temperature around him dropped sharply again and again until Antarctic ice was pricking every inch of Marion's flesh. "God in Heaven, when all is said and done, does not buy you *food*. He does not give you a *house* to call your own. The steeple of the church is the only home for your wife, the only place your children could grow up, and He does not bat an eye at their misfortune. And neither do you." He closed in on the mortal man until he could lean in, draw blood from the bridge of Marion's nose with his own hooked snout, make Marion's facial hair wither with his acidic breath. "You may not think I know humankind," Marion could see every detail of the inside of his mouth: the multiple rows of jagged teeth, the tongue of unfathomable shape and color, and the shapeless black void that led to the wormhole of his throat, "but I do. That is where you are blindly mistaken, *signore*. I know misfortune. I know sadness, hopelessness, fear. I know men. I know *you*. You say you need nothing, that you are happy with the wealth you have been—will be—given, but I know better. I do." He inhaled, and he absorbed the very essence of Marion's life and pulled it into the wormhole. Paralyzed, Marion could do nothing but listen. "I am not blind to suffering, unlike most of mankind." He breathed in again, pulling Marion's energy with him. "You think your wife and children are happy when, in actuality, they suffer every day of their miserable lives. You chose poverty over their happiness, their welfare. For that, and for that alone, I applaud you, for few men could blindly cause their loved ones that much pain. You have given up everything for the wealth you think you'll receive, even the people you love and who love you most. It is truly a sin worthy of my attention. Why not take the next step, *signore*, and offer their flesh, as it was custom so long ago? Or, perhaps, they may offer *themselves* if you keep making them suffer as you do!"

"They would never!"

"Your wife has always resented your decision."

"Poverty has always been resented, but it teaches discipline, and—"

"Poverty teaches *poverty*," the Devil snapped. "It is a leviathan from a deeper level of Hell than even I know."

Marion took several moments to catch his breath, to recapture his life's essence. It created a palpable silence between them. When a portion of his strength returned, Marion replied, "Earthly suffering is only temporary. It creates a deeper appreciation for the reward."

He thought the Devil was going to snap at him again, but

much to his surprise, the specter's smile returned, and his eyes had that certain twinkle once again. "How quaint," he replied with a grin, and even though the torture had ceased, Marion still felt the ice shards of his words scratch and leave bright scars all over his pallid body. "You encourage suffering. It is a ... deeper appreciation for what you say you will have? That sounds like something I would say."

Rage erupted from Marion's soul as he growled, "I will *never* be anything like you."

"Then prove it," the Devil replied, his grin still prominently spread across his face. "Prove you are no longer willing to torture them. End your family's suffering, and end your own. My offer still stands."

"Then I'll take it!" Marion declared in a burst of impulse. As fury kindled the fires of his soul, he had found a way to do the impossible: to trick the Devil, to use his unholy power for *good,* and to conquer the ill of darkness. "But I will not wish for myself or my family alone."

"Suit yourself."

"I will end the suffering for everyone around me. With the power you give me, I will give food—endless food—and a place to store it all, so the hungry can always have their fill. A shelter, a sanctuary, where they can be safe as well as satiated. My family and others will have a home, and it will all be in good will. A soup kitchen, fully staffed, fully stocked, in impressive operation. That is my wish."

The Devil chuckled, but Marion couldn't understand why. Hadn't he just tricked the Devil into doing God's will? Or was there something he was missing?

"I give you my word," the Devil replied. "Your hungry shall have their fill." He grinned. "You will find that I keep my promises, and satisfaction is guaranteed."

*

A long time ago, a small, decrepit house had stood just a few blocks away from the church. Its last owner had died many years before, and since then, the house had been vacant, patiently waiting. For years, it stood ignored, rotting away every second it dared to stand. However, if a pile of wood could hold hope, it certainly did, as while it decayed over the years, it never once showed signs of collapsing. It stood vigilant, ready and willing to accommodate. What warmth remained within those walls, it offered freely, even desperately to those who needed it. After thirty years, though, the house had finally been put out of its long misery. Marion and his wife, with their newborn son, had watched its destruction. For years after, the ghost of the generous old house had remained in the barren lot, though now with no shelter to give.

The morning after Marion's deal with the Devil, though, another building occupied that lot, and no man could feel the joy of the old ghost as it was able to give its resources to the less fortunate once again.

Although the building seemed barely the size of the house before it, the interior was massive. The serving hall alone was about twice the size of the old house as Marion had remembered it. When he went inside, one of the servers found him and ushered him toward two doors in the back of the serving hall. The one on the left, the server said, led to the kitchen, where Marion saw the majority of the workers through a small window in the door. There must have been at least fifty chefs busily preparing food of all types, and there were just as many servers running in and out of the kitchen, politely acknowledging Marion while shoving past him, and there were just as many cleaners tidying up messes from both the chefs and the people being served. Everyone working there was wearing similar—if not the same—white uniforms, and every single worker was inhumanly alert and focused on his or her individual duty. Where all these people had come from, Marion could only guess, but he had a feeling deep in his gut that these people hadn't been "created" by the Devil to serve in his kitchen. The very idea made Marion's stomach turn, but he tried not to let it distract him from the tour.

Now, Marion's guide said, it was time to show him the door on the right, which led to the pantry. Why the pantry needed a room as large as the kitchen, Marion couldn't possibly fathom.

questionMark 55

Until he went inside.

The pantry was not only larger than the kitchen, it seemed to dwarf the building itself! The infinite shelves that towered above him, all filled with food of different kinds, made it look more like a rich man's library than a simple pantry. Bags, boxes, bottles, pitchers, gallons, tins of everything imaginable. Anything and everything edible, from all around the world—even from places Marion had never heard of—was right before his eyes. And it was all his not to take, but to *give*. Marion made his way through each section of the pantry, noticing that everything was immaculately organized, despite the room's size. Anything could be found within minutes if one simply knew where to walk and how high to climb. To Marion's amazement, sections of the room were isolated by temperature so that all the food would be in perfect condition for cooking.

Marion continued to explore until he reached a section where the air around him was not only cold but was as unbearably frigid and piercing as the Devil's glare the night before. He decided to turn back.

His heart skipped several beats as he wandered back through the pantry and noticed chefs climbing ladders, the tops of which Marion could barely see, all around him. A man could climb one of these ladders to reach heaven, Marion thought, but instead of the eternal reward, the chefs reached for various ingredients. He watched as one chef took several boxes from a shelf, but when Marion looked back, the number of boxes hadn't changed, even though the chef held what should have been the whole supply under his arm.

Marion couldn't believe what he was witnessing. He had to see it happen again ... and again ... and again, just to make sure it wasn't a trick of the light.

He watched the same miracle take place throughout the entire pantry; no matter how many chefs came in, no matter how many ingredients they took, the pantry's supply remained exactly the same as it had before. *Infinite food*. It had finally become possible, and it was here that the hungry would finally be fed. The idea of hunger would become a thing of the past. It was here, and it was now. Marion was witnessing one of God's—!

No, he reminded himself. This was not God's work, but only he was allowed to know that. Was this the price he had to pay?

Seeing a row of apples on a bottom shelf, Marion decided to try this miracle for himself, to see if it would work by his own hand. Hesitantly, he reached in and took a brilliant red apple. It was a flawless specimen, perfectly smooth and fresher than any fruit he could possibly afford to buy. Finding himself unable to resist, Marion bit into the apple, and his heart stopped for a time as he relished the taste. It was as perfect and real as it looked and felt, perhaps even more so. What glorious, savory, heavenly flavor came from a single fruit! It couldn't be described with mere words. He couldn't resist eating the rest of the apple until only the core remained (and, had he not stopped himself, he might have been tempted to eat that as well).

Marion looked back at the shelf; indeed, there was another apple, just as glorious and as brilliantly red, in the exact place the first one had been. Marion reached in once more and took the second apple, only to have a third appear in its place. Should he eat this one as well? It was, after all, the exact same as the first one, so it would naturally taste just as perfect … No! He had promised the Devil—such words entering his mind!—he would only use this food to give, not to take. That one apple would be the only food he would eat from this pantry; Marion did not want to be selfish enough to break his promise, as the Devil had made him out to be. Still, he needed to show his wife and children this spectacular food! He needed to show the city, the country, the world!

"Amazing," he breathed, still stunned by the absurdity and the improbability of this magical place. "Today, hunger has been conquered. There will never be an empty stomach in the world again."

*

That very announcement had been made at the church, and from there, the word spread. The poor and hungry came from all over the country to see the soup kitchen for themselves. To their amazement, it was real, and it did exactly what it promised to do: plate after plate, bowl after bowl, the food poured out of the impossible kitchen into the starving bellies of hundreds—no, *thousands*! This was surely the work of God, they said—Marion always affirmed this with a forced smile—a gift from God to all His patient and faithful.

The only thing you could never let them digest, a voice from the back of Marion's mind whispered, *is the truth.*

Despite his guilt, Marion continued to cheerfully lead the workers and invite more people to come and have their fill. He repeatedly affirmed that there would be no one left hungry, no one turned away, as there would always, *always* be enough for everyone.

But would there be? Marion was always on edge; the Devil did say that he would pay at some point for his wish, his gift. But when? What would be the cost?

After only a month in operation, Marion's soup kitchen had fed tens of thousands of people. Word spread to outside the country, and some had spent their entire life's savings on a desperate pilgrimage—a pilgrimage!—to what was said to be God's earthly table. Marion accommodated for every man, woman, and child who came, no matter what language they spoke. They had all heard that a man—a mortal man—named Marion Vive had started a soup kitchen with an unlimited supply of food and where every meal was fit for a king. However, for every blind acceptance from a desperate pilgrim, there were dozens of skeptics who had asked questions about the mysterious kitchen and its endless bounty. Who was this man, Marion Vive, and where had all this food come from? More importantly, what was the secret behind the endless supply?

This phenomenon had gotten the attention of even those too fortunate to require Marion's services. Newspaper writers swarmed from throughout the country and even from surrounding countries to witness the soup kitchen's strange miracle and to try the fantastic food it produced, before recalling their experience to their presses. Word spread even farther and much more quickly. What surprised Marion even more, though, was who *else* decided to investigate: the incredibly wealthy, scientists and doctors, names even a poor man like Marion would have recognized immediately. They, too, were curious about that strange and amazing miracle that was the soup kitchen, and they even requested a meal or two. More astonishing still, they could be accommodated just as easily as any of the poor; the serving hall (quite suspiciously) always had just enough room and, regardless of wealth, there was enough food for *everyone*. However, the most startling part by far was that the food prepared by Marion's soup kitchen even surpassed the expectations of the most privileged, producing far better meals than even the world's greatest chefs could imagine. It was impossible, they said, to make food this delicious and painstakingly prepared in such great supply that it would be available first and foremost to the poor and less fortunate, completely free of charge.

*

Above the serving hall and kitchen, there were large chambers that served as shelters and homes for the poor. The largest and most elegant of the rooms had been given to Marion's family, and every day, Marion would watch his wife gush at the beauty of their new home. She smiled, laughed, even danced more, and he couldn't help but realize this was the happiest she had been in years. Her face was brighter, her cheeks rosier, and Marion knew it wasn't because of the food alone. She talked to him more, showed him more affection, told him how wonderful it was that their lives had changed for the better (not the world around them, but *their* lives), told him how she only wished their son still lived with them so he could share in their good fortune. Ah, well, she concluded, at least their daughters would benefit.

Marion's oldest daughter was reading a book in a soft plush chair while his youngest sat on the floor playing with her cloth dolls. They had both become healthier, his oldest starting to gain a fuller figure and his youngest becoming more excitable, more energetic, apter to run and dance around as she pleased. They had the same rosy cheeks and bright eyes as their mother, and it only made Marion feel guilty.

Had the Devil been right? This question had plagued Marion since the soup kitchen had first manifested, since his wife had first marveled at its majesty and ever-growing renown. He hadn't noticed how much their health had blossomed over the last month alone—he hadn't noticed anything wrong to begin with. But had he really been blind? Had he really been shallow enough in his "discipline" to make them suffer like the Devil said he had? Or was this a trick? Marion didn't know the full extent of the Devil's power, but he assumed he wasn't above manipulating Marion's perception so the mortal man only saw what *he* wanted him to see. It sounded like something the Devil would do, especially to prove his point …

Let's take a walk through the pantry, Papa, his youngest daughter said to him. *I want to walk through the pantry.*

*

One day, about two months later, Marion noticed something: a few spots of brown on the fruit, withering of the vegetable leaves, patches of green on the bread, and a faint stench coming from the meat and fish. The signs of decay were minor, but they were undeniable and impossible to ignore.

Marion stopped one of the chefs who had just taken some of the browned fruit from the shelf. Another fruit, just as brown, materialized in its place. However, Marion wasn't spellbound by the miracle this time.

"You can't use that," he said, putting a hand on the chef's shoulder. "It's going bad. We'll have to throw it out or get fresh fruit somehow."

The chef only gave him a blank stare, although Marion could have sworn there was a faint, familiar twinkle in those dull eyes. "It won't matter. After all, it's not enough to kill anyone. The taste, if anything, will only be *slightly* inferior to what they've grown to expect. But I assure you, no one will notice. No one will care, because these people, they don't ask for much. To them, it's just food."

With that, the chef walked away, his arms full of browned

ingredients that left a faint, faint stench trailing behind him. Marion was baffled, but all he could do now was pray that what the chef had said was true.

*

It had been true, at least for a while.

Marion had kept silent about what he had seen in the pantry. To the hungry, as the chef had predicted, it made no difference. They still scarfed down their food, still acted as though it was the greatest thing they had ever eaten, and even though the wealthy had gradually stopped coming (they were the only ones who had noticed the declining food quality and no longer wished to be associated with the "subpar" kitchen), their absence had been rapidly compensated for. Thousands and thousands of poor filled the hall at a time, climbing over each other, pushing and shoving, all racing toward the nearest available seat. But there was room for everyone.

There was always room.

Marion visited the pantry less and less, fearing what the food would become. Every time he watched the plates and bowls of finished meals pour out of the kitchen, his stomach would always turn a little, but he tried to ignore the growing sense of dread. There was very little wrong with the finished meals at first glance—if he hadn't seen the browned food in the pantry, he wouldn't have known *anything* was wrong—so despite his qualms, Marion continued to stay off to the side.

Until a few months later, when his youngest daughter had eaten and become sick.

She vomited frequently, and though she should have had no appetite, she continued to eat, and every new serving, each subsequent plate made her body deteriorate more and more, but she continued to eat. And each time she ate, she looked up at him with unwavering admiration and bliss—with a pallid, bony face, reddened eyes, and the smell of bile and rot—and said, "Delicious, as always." And she continued to eat.

That was when he interfered.

He tried his best to convince the chefs to throw out and restock the food in the pantry, or at least to prepare something that would help heal his daughter. However, there was no way to give the pantry a fresh supply of food, and anything that could have helped his daughter had now rotted beyond usefulness. Only God could help her now, and given the circumstances, Marion doubted He would.

Despite the pantry's rapid decay, the people kept coming back for more. And more. And more. *And more.*

Even Marion found himself eating the tainted food. It still tasted the same—the brown, shriveled, mushy apple had tasted *exactly* the same as that perfect red specimen he had eaten when he had first gone into the pantry—but his stomach knew better. Horrified, Marion soon stopped eating from the kitchen altogether. It was the only way to stay alive.

Desperate for answers, Marion burst into the pantry, only to find the worst imaginable. Every single piece of food—every bag, every box, every tin, every gallon—was completely rotted away, barely recognizable. Wall to wall, as far across the pantry as he could see and as high up as he could bring himself to look, there was nothing but decay and death. Layers and layers of individual, intertwined stenches filled the room, each one completely identifiable: spoiled meat, rotted fruit, bug-infested vegetables, curdled milk, leafy green and putrid cheese ...

It was not food anymore.

Now, it was dirt and forest. What had not taken root in the walls, floors, and ceiling had rooted itself in the food or turned to mud and caustic sludge, which dripped down the shelves to the floor in front of Marion's feet.

And there was still an infinite supply.

Infinity rotted on those shelves. Mold choked the whole room, flies taunted him, sludge drowned him, ate him alive, and still, the chefs took the food and obliviously—or did they know full well what they were doing?!—prepared it as another nightmare took the place of each one removed, exactly the same as, if not worse than, before.

"Stop! *Stop*!" He fell to his knees, stopping one of the chefs in his path. "Please, stop it! Stop it! It's terrible, all of this is terrible!

Please! Someone will die, I tell you! Someone will die if you don't stop cooking this! Someone will die! Please, for the love of God, stop!"

Marion continued to beg, but the chefs didn't even flinch, not even the one to whose ankle Marion clung for dear life.

"Don't blame us," the chef above Marion said in a chilling monotone. "They are the ones desperate enough to eat the food we prepare. If they did not want to eat, they would have stopped coming."

"But they will still eat," another nearby chef continued, his arms full of sludge and clouds of blossoming mold. "They want to escape the suffering you say will discipline them, will make them appreciate their reward. They claw their way out of the pit, destroying each other in the process. They are savage. They only want to survive. You, too, Marion Vive. Even you eat the food we prepare, despite its 'condition.' Tell me, does it really make a difference? Does it really taste different at all? You may say it does, but *they* don't. It is still food to them, and they eat."

"It turns out, Marion Vive," a third chef chimed in, "that not everyone is as disciplined as you. They do not see poverty as you do. They see it as *he* does."

"They are gluttonous by nature, and so are you," the second chef added, "although you would have been much better off wishing for personal wealth. There would not have been nearly as much blood on your hands."

"But it wasn't my fault! I didn't plan for the food to rot! I didn't plan for the people to get sick!"

"You should have expected it," the third chef replied. "After all, it was an infinite supply, but nothing *lasts* forever. All things must die. All things must rot. All things, though they remain on this earth, must fall to the worm and soil. A man with true discipline would have known that."

"Alas," another chef stated, "there is no discipline here. There never has been. Man, above all, is an animal, and nature is not bound by discipline. There is only one thought, and that is food. If it is edible, then it is eaten. Wouldn't you agree, Marion Vive?"

"But it isn't!" Marion exclaimed, still clutching the chef's ankle. "It … It shouldn't be!"

"But it is. They think so, so it becomes."

The first chef narrowed his eyes as he looked down at Marion with that icy glare. That icy glare, it had haunted him since the soup kitchen had first materialized. That icy glare, he felt it from all around him, from not only the chefs and the flies but the food itself. The food, the sludge and plants and fluffy, fluffy clouds, it all had eyes, the eyes of a thousand tortured souls, closing in, strangling him, pulling the air out of his lungs as the denizens of Hell passed their judgment.

"Remember, you have dealt with the Devil," the chef above him stated, the entire chorus of the damned spilling out of that one mouth. "And satisfaction is guaranteed."

*

There must have been tens of thousands of people in the serving hall, all shoving past each other, all screaming and yelling, all piling on top of an empty spot—even though there was still room, there was always room—all fighting for the right to sit down and eat rancid sludge. The people who were already eating were fighting back, defending their territory. Realizing that their attempts were becoming fruitless, some of them turned their attention to the kitchen and pantry; why steal from someone else when one could steal from the source? They rushed, climbing over and shoving past one another, toward the back of the serving hall. The only thing that stopped the stampede was Marion standing in front of the kitchen door, blocking their path.

"Get out! Get out of here!" he yelled over the war-cries and agonizing screams of the rest of the crowd. "We can't serve you anymore! Leave, while you still can! I'm sorry, we have to close!"

"Why?" a man who had been eating at the kitchen since it had first opened (Marion felt guilty for recognizing him) asked. "You said you would never turn anyone away. Are you going back on your word? Why now?"

"The food ..." Marion was about to explain the whole story when he thought better of it. If they knew the truth, they would think he was absolutely crazy, especially if the food was still somehow as delicious as ... Marion didn't want to think about that. "Please, I ... I don't have time to explain. Just ... please, please believe me."

"What about the food?" a woman shouted. She looked more like a banshee than anything human, with long, shaggy hair and a near skeletal body. "It's fine! It's always been!"

"But it's not! Please, it's terrible. My daughter has gotten sick because of it, and so have several others. Please, you don't understand, I'm asking you to do this for your own good! Get out of here, and if you know what's best for you, please don't come back until—!"

The crowd began to rumble, soon drowning out Marion's speech. To his dismay, it quickly grew into an uncontrollable roar.

"You're making excuses!"
"Changing your mind? Keeping it all for yourself?"
"Cockroach!"
"Give us the food!"
"I'm starving!"
"You slimy bastard!"
"Give us all this food, and you take it away like that!"
"Go to Hell!"
"I spent months traveling—!"
"Let the cooks do their job, for God's sake!"
"How dare you!"
"My family is starving!"
"Son of a bitch!"

A riot soon rose, and Marion had no choice but to move out of the way. They stormed the kitchen and pantry, which strangely didn't faze the workers, and from those rooms rose commotion that normally would have drowned out the rest of the noise. But there was more than enough noise in the serving room, more than enough to drive Marion insane.

They ate, and ate, and ate, and ate, and ate, and Marion was tortured by every last cry for more food, and as the food left the kitchen and pantry, it grew progressively worse. And worse. And worse. And worse.

Even from where Marion was cowering, he could see the final stage of this disastrous phenomenon: when they had eaten more than enough of the mud and sludge, each patron's face had turned a different color—mostly green or red, although there were some spots of blue and deathly pale scattered among the crowd. Each had the misfortune of their own sickness: some began with acidic stomach pains, some vomited profusely, some choked, some writhed, some fainted. The weakest ones had been fortunate enough to die right away, although their frail and poisoned bodies were taken back to the kitchen to be used for a variety of pork-based dishes.

And those who were still alive and writhing, they *still* ate! They screamed and howled for more food and were not too proud to eat the expertly-prepared corpses of their peers, which in turn tainted their own meat more and more as that gruesome cycle of life continued. At the very worst they could have been while still alive (and *still* could eat), they crawled along wormlike on the ground through the vomit and excretions of their brethren, begging for more, more, more food despite the toll it had taken. They shrieked and screeched, continued to beg, continued to demand more, more, *more*! They were no longer human; sordid meat-worms, they would willingly eat themselves to death if they hadn't died already.

Only the strong-willed and strong-bodied were left at this point, and they continued to gorge themselves, so desperate in their desire—their *lust*—for more food that a few even tried to eat Marion alive! He had to fight to keep the hungry men off his legs, off his body. He climbed as high as he could, warding them away with whatever weapons he could find. The creatures were revolting enough when they were fighting over what carcass and sludge would be their next meal, but when they were trying to skin and devour living meat? Marion was relieved when they had become distracted by some rats, some new competitors that had wandered inside. Those unfortunate creatures, though, had been gobbled up in an instant, although whether or not they had been killed first was up to the personal preference of the worm.

Marion couldn't bear to watch. At first, he thought he had been doing the work of God by feeding all those people, but now ... now, he was able to say that he had seen Hell. In front of his eyes—the floors stained with corpses and psychedelic blood, vomit, and acid; the worms who were left, having realized that Marion was no longer worth fighting for and that no more rats dared to wander into the building, now trying to eat *each other* to determine who would get the next green, sludgy meal—was what only could be described as Hell. And Marion couldn't bear it. He couldn't take it anymore.

He wanted to escape the clutches of this leviathan, to climb out of the pit.

But how? How could he redeem himself in the eyes of God, whom he had betrayed? How could he beg for forgiveness when he was only a single blemish in the sea of harlequin splatters?

Without another word or thought, Marion ran into the pantry, where he searched the even more grotesque room for some spare materials ...

Satisfaction guaranteed, said the Devil in the back of his mind as Marion found what he needed and climbed the nearest ladder, *but I never said yours.*

*

Marion's youngest daughter, along with the rest of his family, had also died. Whether it had been before or after his suicide, no one knew. The entire soup kitchen was deserted: the serving hall, the kitchen, the chambers and, of course, the rotting pantry. If foul play of some kind had been involved, there was no evidence to prove it; every room except the pantry was spotless. No staff remained, and no patrons remained, either. The soup kitchen was as barren as the house that had preceded it, although from the new rumors that had begun to circulate since the soup kitchen's "closing," the generous old house had far, far better intentions.

The only clue that remained to the source of Marion Vive's agony was the note he had hastily written on parchment in what smelled like pig's blood, and whatever the makeshift writing utensil had been was now deeply embedded in the piece of sordid meat the blood had come from.

This, it had been revealed to those who had found Marion's body and the rotted pantry, was what the note read:

My dear friends,

I know I have dealt with the Devil, and disaster has come from it like nothing I have ever imagined. My soul is tarnished now; I had tried to trick the Devil and had not succeeded. That creature with whom I had bargained told me I would pay for my wish in time, and with my immortal soul, I have.

I can no longer walk on this earth with a clean conscience. I cannot close my eyes without seeing the horrors that transpired here. I cannot look upon the face of God without knowing He will turn His back on me. My only rest is in Hell, visions of which I have seen here, and where I am destined to fall. Let my demise serve as a reminder to those who should come that if they are hungry, they should not eat from this pantry.

Eric Manchester Takes His Medicine

She's been spying on me. I know it. I can see her looking through the window at me. I would know her anywhere. She's trying to figure out what's going on.

She's trying to see what happened to my parents.

My parents have been sick for almost a year now. I can't save them. I can only take care of them, give them medicine, and they look like they're getting better. I've been taking medicine myself. I can go to school and not worry about infecting other people, but my parents can't leave the house. They'd infect the whole town, and the whole town would die, and it'd just be me left. I'm fine, I'll always be fine, but I still need to take the medicine.

You can't be too careful.

You need to have friends, Eric, Mother would say. It's not healthy for a young man to go through high school by himself.

Father hates to see me unhappy like this. Slaving over them, taking care of them, making sure the disease doesn't kill them. He says I need to do something for myself every once in a while. That I've become stressed. More tense. Paranoid, even.

But I'm fine, I tell them. I've always been fine. I don't need friends. I don't need to do anything for myself because my life is here. My life is here with you, taking care of you, making sure you get better because I can't lose you. Not now. Not ever.

Mother is sitting on the couch watching TV. She can't be bothered to change the channel. Out of the corner of my eye, I can see Britt watching me from the window. I would know her anywhere. We have chemistry—and English together. From what I can see of her, she looks beautiful today, but that's not important. I'm sure it's her that's watching me. Should I say something? Should I do something? No, I don't say anything to the other people who've been watching. I don't do anything to the people who stop me, threaten me, demand to know what's going on and keep demanding it until I tell them what they want to hear. They keep asking me, though I've already told them the truth. Horrible people. Horrible, horrible people.

But Britt is the least horrible of them.

I help Mother back into the bedroom—I have to help them everywhere now—and I notice Father's in a bad mood. He's been noticing the people spying on us, too.

If I didn't feel like shit, he says, I'd go out and get those bastards off our property myself. Why do they even come here? Don't they have any sense of privacy? Any sense of respect?

I agree. I'd offer to go out and chase them away myself, but I don't want to do that. I don't want to call any more attention to ourselves, make ourselves look more suspicious because that's what *they* want us to do. They want us to be aggressive, to give them an excuse to break into our house and take everyone away, to make *me* look like a freak. They want to make me look like I deserve everything I'm getting for trying to help my family, and they want to lock me up, lock me up forever because I locked *myself* up, locked myself away and everyone wanted to know why, why I did, what I was hiding—!

I comfort Father and tell him everything's going to be alright. Is it, though? I don't know, but that's what I tell him. Then, I notice the house smells terrible. I need to spray it down again. I've been using a lot of air freshener lately, and if I don't go out and get more soon, I'm going to run out, and the house will start to stink again, but it's okay. It's a regular thing, a thing that happens. The smell is just part of the disease. It's horrible, but I have to put up with it so that someday, they'll be cured.

But I need to take my medicine. You can't be too careful.

*

I sit in tenth period English and try to keep up, but my thoughts keep going back to my parents. My eyes don't leave the textbook. I read every word, I understand every word, I picture every word in my head, but I can't stop thinking about them. It's impossible not to think about them. Are they okay? What if someone knew I was gone and broke into the house, if they saw my parents and got the wrong idea, if they took them away and I came home to an empty house full of people waiting to take me away, too, because they didn't understand? Because I tried to tell them what was wrong and they didn't listen? They wouldn't listen, I know they wouldn't, and because they wouldn't, they'd get the disease and spread it! Spread it to everyone who spies on us, everyone who interrogates me and refuses to believe the truth, just so they know how it feels, spread it to the rest of the town because they don't understand, they don't help, and they all deserve to suffer. They all deserve to suffer for what they've done! They all need to suffer! And then I'll be the only one left alive, I'll be the only one unharmed, I'll be the only one feeling well because I take my medicine, I take my medicine and I don't get sick! I don't get sick! I'm not—!

I need to focus. I need to stop thinking about them for a while, about the disease. I need to relax. Mother said so. I'm going to try.

The bell rings, and I get my books and head for the door. I'm trying not to think about them. I'm trying to relax. I'm trying not to jitter, trying not to fidget, I just need to get to the door and out of the room and out of the—

Oof!

My books fly out of my arms as I run into someone, and as I kneel down to pick them up, I hear a voice.

Oh, hey ... sorry, Eric.

I look up as I get half my books in order. It's her. I know it. I would know her anywhere. She's trying to interrogate me, trying to figure out what happened to my parents, trying to figure out

questionMark 71

what's going on so she can tell everyone else, so they can take us away and destroy everything, everything—! Or not. She only said hi. Hi? That's not the start of an interrogation. That's not the start of anything. That's the start of a ... a conversation. Huh.

'S okay, I mumble, still looking up at Britt. I get all my books together and stand up. I'm just a little taller than her, and I'm able to look into her eyes. They're brown, deep brown. I haven't got this good a look at them before. The books start to slip out of my grasp as I immediately ask, You're not going to ask about my parents, are you? Just like everyone else?

They call it a knee-jerk reaction, me saying that, and I've probably offended her, for all I know, but I have to make sure. I need to make sure so I can get it out of the way, to let her know that if she *was* here to interrogate me, it's not going to happen. I won't answer any questions, I won't give any information, and I'm sorry, but she is not allowed inside the house for any reason because she would get the disease, it's highly contagious and I would let her share my medicine, I really would, but I only have enough to last me until the end of the month, and that's the only time I can get more, so no, she cannot come in the house, I'm—!

No, I, uh, I just wanted to know how you were doing.

How—How I'm doing? How do I answer that? No, you are not allowed in the house—no, that's not it.

I must look confused because she corrects herself, Um, how are you keeping up with school? You know, with, uh, everything that's going on?

She knows. I know she's been watching because she knows. How else would she know? How else? Or maybe she heard about it, or maybe some other reason. Everyone knows, anymore. It's nothing new, but that still doesn't get her off scot-free, doesn't make me any less suspicious of her.

I've been doing alright, I say. I mean, I get by, if that's what you're asking.

I know she's going to ask about my parents. If not now, then soon. We may as well get it over with because I know I saw her, I would know her anywhere. She can't deny it. She can't tell me that she doesn't want to know the truth because I saw her and she can't tell me she wasn't there because she was there, I saw her. I'm not falling for it, whatever it is. I won't talk.

Okay, she replies, because, um, I know something like that can be, uh, hard on you. Like, really hard. Well, I mean, uh, if you were having any trouble, you know, with your ... being busy and all that, if you needed any help, you know, I could ... ?

She could what? Ask about my family? Ask about the house? Try to go there? Try to get me to talk, even though I'm not going to talk, I'll never talk no matter how much she tries to get me to, I'll never—!

... I could, maybe, help out? Only if you want me to, though. You, uh ... You look like you have a lot on your plate, so, uh ...

I don't know how to react. She ... she's being nice. At least, I think she's being nice. She could still be trying to bait me, trying to get my guard down, trying to ... what is she trying to do? I wish I could read her mind, figure out what she's trying to say, but I'm struggling with my own as it is. I wish I knew what to say. Looking at her, I wish I could believe her. I wish I could believe she means what she says, that she's not lying to me, she's not planning to betray me later to the people who want an excuse to lock me up and never let me see my family again. Is this what talking's like? Is this what it's supposed to be? I want to believe, but Father's right, I'm getting paranoid. Paranoid. It's strange to sum up everything I'm feeling in just that one word, that one nasty word, but they'll thank me later. Everyone will thank me later.

No, it's fine, I say. Everything's going fine now. But thank you, thanks for offering.

No problem, she says. Well, uh, the offer's always open if, you know, things get a little too hard. Y'know, Eric, she adds as I try to leave, it's kind of a shame no one talks to you. Y'know, tries to get to know you a little more. I mean ... you sound like a ... a really interesting person.

I look over my shoulder to face her again. What is she trying to pull? What kind of torture is this? Really? I ask.

She looks like she's caught in a lie. Is she, or is there another reason she's as nervous as I am?

Yeah, she replies after a moment. I mean, I've never met anyone like you before, if that, uh, if that says anything.

Is that good? I feel stupid for asking. I almost forget the

questionMark 73

possibility that, yes, she may still be using this tactic to get information about my parents, about the disease. Almost.

I guess it's good, Britt replies. I mean—I'm not trying to make fun of you, if that's what ... er ... I know you're going through a lot of hard times, if what you're saying about your family is true, and ... I guess what I'm trying to say is that school doesn't exactly help with that, from what I've seen. Plus—again, given what you're saying is true because I don't know for sure—if it is true, then ... I guess what I'm saying is that you're really brave. If what you're saying is true, I mean.

If it's true? It's always been true. Why would she have any doubt? Because she hasn't been there—no, she's been there, she's been spying through my window, she's been there, but she doesn't know. She doesn't know what it's like, she doesn't know what I go through, what my family goes through ... and should she know? No, I wouldn't like her to know firsthand, I wouldn't like her to get the disease, but if she's lying to me, if she betrays me, if she's only doing this to get my guard down, then yes, she'll get the disease and help it spread all throughout town, and she'll die like the rest of them, but it wouldn't stop me from being sad about it for a while because I've never met anyone else like her, either.

Thank you, I reply. I don't know what else to say. I don't know if there's anything else to say.

Hey, listen, Britt says, I know you're busy and all, but, um, maybe if you have a night free, maybe you could, um ... maybe we could, I dunno, we could maybe go eat at—

No.

No, I can't do that. It's a trap, it's definitely a trap. No matter what she said before, no matter what she's trying to say now, she's trying to get me as far away from the house as possible so I can't defend my family in case anything happens, in case she tells those horrible people we're gone and they're free to do what they want because I won't be around, in case they take Mother and Father away and come after me next, and my life would fall apart from there, and God help everyone else—!

I'm sorry, I reply. I can't do that. I-I wish I could, but my parents need me. I need to be at home. They need me, but I wish I could, I really do. Trust me, this is for the better. This is for the better. This is for the better.

She looks surprised. I have foiled her plot. I am victorious. We will be safe another day.

Well, I mean, she adds, I didn't say *tonight*, I mean, well, whenever you're free …

I ignore her as I celebrate my victory. She does seem nice, though, but how nice? Nice enough to not be like everyone else, to not lie to my face in hopes of getting the information she needs in order to destroy me, destroy us, destroy everything? I don't trust that because that's all that happens whenever someone tries to talk to me. The ulterior motive is always the same. After all, no one talked to me before, so why are they talking to me now? Why not then, and why now? Because they want to know. They want to know everything, and they want to be destroyed, and she's no different. Why hasn't she talked to me before? Why did she choose now to talk to me? Because, because …

I don't know why, but I'm glad she did.

I head outside, not even bothering to look back at her. I like talking to her, I realize. I like the sound of her voice. I want to keep her around because someone else to talk to is always good. Mother says I should have friends, but there's too much of a risk. There's too much of a risk involved, but based on how that conversation with Britt went, is it worth it? What I felt, what I heard her say, what I said, what I'm feeling now—is it worth all that? Yes. It is.

Maybe just one friend. One friend will be enough for now.

I head straight home.

*

You're looking better. How are you feeling? I ask Mother and Father when I get home.

Fine, Mother says. The fever still hasn't gone, but we're managing.

I caught some more people spying earlier, Father adds. They're damn lucky—!

Just let it go, Henry, Mother says. Stressing about it is only going to make it worse. I thought you knew that by now.

Mother's right, I say as I sit on the edge of their bed. You need to get more rest. Try to relax for a while. You need me to get you anything?

Nah, Father says. I'm fine. Glass of water, maybe, but that's it. My throat's been feeling a little dry, but I don't want to bother you too much. You got much homework, kid?

Not much, I reply. Should I turn on the TV?

There's not much on, Mother replies.

That's fine. I have big news for them, anyway. The TV shouldn't be on. I go get Father a glass of water and put my books away. When I get back with the water, Father thanks me, but he doesn't touch it.

You take your medicine today, Eric? Mother asks. Mother's always concerned about me and my medicine. She wants to make sure I stay healthy, too.

Not yet, I reply. I was going to take some before I did my homework tonight. I have a timer set, I always do. Did you forget?

Well, no, I know you always take it on time, but, Eric, she says, I'm asking because you've been looking really pale lately. Are you sure you're alright? Maybe you've been overdosing or something—

Give the kid a break, Father says. He's been following the label, how can he be overdosing? Diana, the kid's fine. Stop worrying about him so much.

Father's right, I say. I feel fine. Would you feel better if I told you what happened at school today?

Mother chuckles. Well, this is a change. We usually have to ask.

I'm excited. I wonder what they'll think.

A girl talked to me today, I tell them. Right after school. I don't know if it was an accident or on purpose, but she didn't ask about us or the disease like everyone else does. She—she wanted to get to know me. She said I was interesting, said I was the—that she hadn't met anyone else like me before, and it's a surprise because no one asks about me. No one ... no one wants to get to know me, especially not now, and it's ... I don't know, I can't describe how it feels. I just know that, well, I know that she's different. I don't know how I know that, but just from talking to her …

Father chuckles. Well, it's about time you came home with something like this. I was starting to get worried. You're, what, a junior now?

I chuckle sheepishly in reply.

Tell me everything, he adds.

She's very quiet, I reply. I mean, she doesn't talk to anyone else. She's not popular like Leila George was, but she's very attractive, at least to me. And she asked me to eat somewhere with her, too.

Are you going to go? Mother asks.

No, I reply, because I need to stay here with you. I need to take care of you, to protect you from the people spying outside, the people who want to take us away. If I'm not here, then who's going to stop them from coming in?

We'll be fine for one night if you want to go, Mother says.

And you do wanna go, Father adds, or else you've just turned down a date, son, and girls tend not to like that.

That's true. I bite my lip. I don't want to lose my only friend right after I met her, but I still want to protect my family in case it's a trap and she *is* lying to me. What do I do?

Give her a chance, Mother says as if she's read my mind. If she really does like you for who you are, then it'll be worth it. That's what I've been trying to tell you since the beginning. You need a break, Eric. You need some time away. It'll be good for you. We'll be fine, honey. We'll be fine for one night.

I hope so.

Whether you like it or not, kiddo, you're growing up, Father says, grinning. Soon, you won't need us anymore.

I don't want that to happen.

I go and spray down the house again before taking my medicine. You can't be too careful.

*

It's been a few weeks since I first talked to Britt, and not once has she asked about my parents. Not once has she tried to interrogate me. We talk in class, between classes, and right after school, which usually makes me about twenty minutes late to get home, but Mother and Father don't mind. They're actually happy for me. They want me to be late. Not too late, as they'd get worried that something's happened to me, but late enough that I'm not always home at two forty-five on the dot each day. It's weird.

I finally agree to go out and eat with her. Friday night, 6:00 at Ziara's Diner. Of course, I had to schedule it in advance because I needed to ask Mother and Father first, but they let me go. I'm surprised they let me go. I wash my clothes for the first time in months. I take a shower, brush my hair ... I try to make myself look halfway presentable—but what's presentable? I don't know. All I know is that I look a little better than I usually do, and if that's enough, then it's enough.

I lock all the windows. I pull down the blinds and shades before nailing the curtains to the wall and sewing them shut. I lock the side and back doors (*Click-click-click-click-click-click-click. Click-click-click-click-click-click-click*) before shoving a table or dresser against them so no one gets any ideas. Before I leave, I lock the front door behind me (*Click-click-click-click-click-click-click-click-click-click*) and look for any possible entrances I forgot to block off. When everything's secured, I head toward the restaurant.

Britt's already there. For a moment, I worry that I'm late, since I spent so much time securing the house, but it turns out that she came early, too. She's wearing a blouse, the nicest blouse I've ever seen. Am I overdressed? Am I underdressed? She doesn't seem to mind either way. She's glad I came. I smile a little. I'm feeling a little better already.

We sit down at our table. I'm a little ashamed to tell Britt that I've never been here before (or, if I have, I don't remember it very much), and she's all right with it. She says she comes here all the time, and she gives me her recommendations—the chicken basket, the best bacon double cheeseburger in town, the wings, the fish-n-chips, and she also tells me about the root beer floats, how they're completely homemade.

After dinner, she orders a float for each of us, and when I try some of mine, it's absolutely delicious. I can't remember the last time I had something like this, especially something I haven't had to make myself. It relaxes me and makes me more nervous at the same time—I can't explain it. We talk a little more, and as we talk, I start to remember my life before my parents got sick. I think back to what my hobbies were before, what I liked to do, what I would have talked about if I had any friends, and then I realize that it seems like a lifetime ago. It's only been about a year, though, and that's what strikes me. I've changed more than I thought, but I feel like I have a good reason for it. I've changed, but everyone will thank me. Everyone will thank me—!

How are your parents feeling?

The question is casual, so casual, and yet alarms are going off in my head. She did ask about them. She *did* ask. What does this mean? Has she been lying to me this whole time? Does she really only care about the house and about the disease and about the—?

Better, I say. They've been feeling a little better, but it's gradual.

Oh, okay, she replies. I just wanted to make sure because from what you said, it seemed kind of bad. I might send a card or something sometime this week.

I frown. This isn't the response I was expecting. Sympathy? Or is she making fun of me? Is she making fun of the fact that I need sympathy? The fact that I need—and that's when I remember that I forgot to take my medicine before I left. I remind myself to take it when I get home, but I can't help but wonder what'll happen if I miss a dose. Will I get sick? I might need to take extra to make up for missing …

They seem like nice people, Britt adds. At least, from what you've told me about them.

They are, I reply. I'm sure they'd appreciate a card.

I take a sip of my root beer float. So does she. Maybe I'm worrying too much. Maybe I should just enjoy myself—because I am. I am enjoying myself. I take another sip.

This is really refreshing.

*

questionMark

Another week passes, and Britt and I are really good friends now. We talk often, and I'm starting to trust her. Maybe, just maybe, she might be able to come into the house. It's been a while since we've had company. I'm sure Mother and Father will enjoy it. After all, they enjoyed the card that Britt gave me to give to them. The medicine ... I might be able to split it. Maybe. I don't know how much I'll need, though, and I don't know how much she'll need. Plus, I'll need to spray down the house again. I need to spray it down or else it'll stink, and she'll get the wrong idea. She'll be just like everyone else, and then she'd call the people to take me, take us away—!

Or she could stay as far away from the house as possible. We could go out for lunch or dinner every single day for the rest of our lives and it would be fine as long as she went nowhere near the house. That way, things would be better. Everyone would be safe. But she wants me to trust her, I can tell. She's let me see her house, and even though her parents were scared of me, criticized her for even talking to me, I know she wanted them to trust me, too. She trusts me. Me, the crazy one, and I feel like I have to do the same for her.

Not to mention, Mother and Father have been really lonely. I tried to tell myself it's not true, but it is. They're locked up inside the house because of me, even though I did it for their own good. They haven't seen anyone new in months. I know they're not happy, especially Mother. She was very excited when I told her about Britt and ... she encouraged me to ask her. Let her inside the house. Let her meet them because they've been lonely.

We can always get more medicine, she says. Besides, I feel like you've been taking too much of it lately, and it's starting to affect your health. I think you need this.

Maybe I do, but I'm healthy. I've always been healthy, and I'm not sick. And you can't be too careful. You can't be too careful.

But I ask her anyway. Another week later, right after third period chemistry.

Just you, I tell her. No one else.

Sure, she replies. I'd love to.

She hesitated—what does that mean? I know what it means. It means this isn't the first time she's been there. It means she's been spying, spying as she's done in the past. She thinks I don't know, but I do—I do, and I'm going to call her out on it when she gets there, when she's too familiar with it or she acts like it's the first time she's been when she's been there before, she's been there before, and she thinks I'm too stupid, I'm too stupid to see through—!

No. That's not going to happen because Britt wouldn't try to investigate. I feel it in my gut. Is this what it's like to trust someone? I know for a fact she wouldn't try to investigate because she's never, not once, interrogated me. Maybe it's not her that I keep seeing outside the house because I know she wouldn't do that to me. Maybe it's someone else, someone who looks like her.

How about today after school? I ask, before adding, Are you free?

She hesitates—what does that mean? My heart is racing. Maybe it's too soon. Maybe I should have said next week, next month, given her time to prepare, maybe to ask her parents or something if it's alright. Of course, they'll say no because they hate me, they don't want her to have anything to do with me, but would she still have to ask? Would they have to know where she is—?

Yeah, sure, she replies. I'm good after school.

I don't know what to think.

*

I walk home with Britt, and my heart is still pounding. I'm not sure what she's thinking as we approach the house. She's probably having second thoughts. Right about now, she's probably making up an excuse, maybe that she forgot something or that she forgot she had to go somewhere else with someone else, anything to get her away from me, away from here—or does she want to keep going? She's still following me—why? Does she want to meet my parents—or does she want to investigate? Is she using this as a means to investigate the house, to interrogate me, to get me at my weakest, at my most vulnerable, and take me away, take everyone away and destroy everything? For a moment, I consider changing my mind. I'm having second thoughts, too, and I almost give an excuse to be somewhere else, but it's too late now. It's too late. We're already there.

Do you smell something? Britt asks.

It's too late. Too late. Too late.

Smell what? I reply.

It smells like ... like something died here.

It gets like that every so often, I reply. I hate it. I have to spray the house down to get rid of it, but it never goes away. It's just ... it's just something that happens.

She's looking at me funny. I look suspicious, I realize. I'm drawing attention to myself, even if it's just from her. My heart feels like it's about to burst. I've made a terrible mistake, but it's too late, too late to turn around and go back and eat somewhere and pretend this never happened because we're already here, we're already standing in front of the house. She's looking at the ten locks on the front door. No doubt she's wondering why I use ten locks to lock the front door—maybe, I think she's thinking, maybe they're right about him, maybe he is crazy—but I'm not. I'm not crazy, she just doesn't understand. I need to make her understand. I need to make her see *why*, I need to make her see that they're sick, that the disease is real, and that I'm not crazy. I've never been crazy. I'm perfectly healthy.

Mother's looking forward to meeting you, I say as if nothing had happened.

I unlock the front door.

Click.

My hands are trembling.

Click-click-click.

Click-click.

Every once in a while, I look over my shoulder to see if she's still there. She's still there.

Click.

Click-click.

She's still looking at me funny. Probably because I've been looking over my shoulder so much.

Click.

We go inside.

The house is a mess. I forgot to clean it. I should have scheduled this for next week or next month after all so I would have had time to prepare. This was a mistake. It was a mistake. This was a bad idea ...

My medicine is in the kitchen, I tell her before leading her there. You can have some. It'll protect you while you're here.

And it won't work on your parents? Britt asks.

They're too far gone, I reply. I've tried it. All I can do now is take care of them, try to make them feel better for as long as I can. There's no cure right now, none that I know, but I believe there'll be one someday, and I'm willing to wait that long because I don't want to lose them. They're all I have, Britt. They're all I have.

Eric ... Eric, you're starting to creep me out.

But you understand, don't you? You're the only one who's believed me. I've tried to tell them, but no one believes me. The smell comes, they say the same thing you did about it, and they talk. They think my parents are dead, Britt. That's what they think. They think I'm ... I'm trying to hide them or something, that's what they keep saying, and it's not true. They're not dead. They're still here. They're just sick, that's all. The smell, it comes from the disease. The disease is what's making the smell, making them look the way they do, not because they're dead. I keep trying to explain it and no one listens, no one knows, no one understands that I would do absolutely anything to keep them safe. Th-there's the medicine. I'll get you some water, you can take some. I want to keep you safe. I want to keep them safe because I love them, I would do absolutely anything for them. You understand, don't you?

Eric, are you okay?

... I feel fine.

She doesn't say anything else for a while. She just looks at the old refrigerator, the sink filled with dishes, and the kitchen table covered in pills. *Pills, pills, everywhere, more than enough to be immune, completely immune, at least for now until the new bottles come in the mail.*

But she leaves them alone. She doesn't touch them. Why? She's taking a very big risk—I make sure she knows that—but she doesn't seem to mind.

questionMark

It's her loss. You can't be too careful.

I show her to the bedroom. The TV is off, and my parents are in their bed right where I left them. I know they're excited, especially Mother. They wanted to see her, and I hope she likes them …

*

I don't know why she's scared.

I don't know why she's yelling at me, telling me I lied to her. I didn't. I told her the truth, I told everyone the truth, but they didn't believe me, and neither does she. She's just like everyone else after all. I don't know why I thought this was a good idea. This was the biggest mistake I've ever made in my life, and now I'm going to pay for it. Everyone is going to pay for it.

What's wrong? Mother asks.

Britt doesn't answer her.

She tells me they're dead, but they're not dead.

Their skin is sagging, their eyes are glazed over, and I know this. I know all of this. I try to clean them up and make them look decent, try to make them not look like skeletons, try to make them feel better about themselves but it never works, and it's all part of the disease. It's all part of the disease, and she doesn't believe me. She's never believed me, no one has ever believed me.

And now she's going to leave, say the rumors are true, call the people to take me away. Take us away. I can't let that happen. I can't let her destroy my family, what's left of it. I can't let her insult me, insult us, destroy me, destroy everything—!

The stench is unbearable. I can tell she's about to faint. It's part of the disease, it doesn't mean they're dead. She's just like everyone else after all. She was just like everyone else.

She's still yelling at me. She's telling me I'm sick. I'm not sick. I'm perfectly healthy, perfectly fine because I take my medicine. I'm not sick. I'm not sick. You can't be too careful, you can't be too careful, I can't be too careful. Can't be too careful.

She keeps telling me to stop lying, stop denying it, but I'm not denying it—they're right there in front of me, alive! Alive! I try to tell her again and again, but she won't have it. She doesn't believe me. She'll never believe me. She says they're dead, and they've always been dead, and they've never been alive for me to take care of, but it's not true! It's not true! It's not true!

She tells me the truth. She'd decided to give me a chance. I looked like I was nice and the rumors couldn't possibly be true. She thought I was nuts—she knew I was nuts, she didn't believe for a second that I wasn't—but she didn't think I was capable of anything like that, hiding them away, locking them up, denying it to everyone who asked. She wanted to investigate for herself—I would know her anywhere, she was the one, she was the one standing outside and looking in through the window and—but she wanted to believe me. She wanted to know that they *were* sick, and she wanted to fight for me. She wanted to support me because … because she liked me.

But now she doesn't. I'd proven her wrong, even though I'm right and I've always been right and she doesn't believe me even though she does, she said she did. She doesn't understand even though she said she did, she thought she did. I can't let her leave. She wants me taken away—she's screaming that now—she wants me taken away and my family taken away and I don't want that to happen, I don't want that to happen.

If she gets her way, I'll never see my family again. I don't want that to happen.

I stand there and look at her. I plead with her. I try to make her understand, but she won't listen. I keep trying. I don't want them to take me away. Please don't let them take me away. Please. I don't want to go. I want to stay with my family. I want to take care of them because I would do absolutely anything for them, absolutely anything, and I'm not sick! I'm not sick because I take my medicine, and I'll keep taking it as long as it takes, as long as it takes for them to be cured because I don't want to lose them, I never want to lose them! I want to stay with them forever, help them feel better because—!

I'm on the floor, sobbing. I've destroyed the room, thrown everything. My parents are ashamed of me. I can hear them scolding me, telling me I shouldn't have done that, that I needed to be on my best behavior because we have a guest in the house,

questionMark

the first guest in so many months. I've embarrassed them. I've been acting like a child. I curl up, pressing some of the broken glass against my legs, cutting them, making them bleed all over my pants.

The police are probably on their way. I barely heard her call. I'm helpless now, as vulnerable as my parents are. I've failed. I couldn't protect them.

She's running away now. I could stop her, but that would bring too much attention to myself. That's what *they* would want me to do. They want to make me look like I deserve it, like I deserve what I'm getting. They want me to look like a freak. She wants me to look like a freak. Besides, I can't move. I can't bring myself to move. I can only lay here in a pool of my own blood until they drag me away.

They're not dead, I whimper as I hear noise from downstairs. Crashing. Shouting. They're inside.

Eric!
Eric ...
I can't move.
They're not dead.
Get up, Eric.
I can't.
They're coming up the stairs.
They're coming for us, Eric.
They're not dead.
I need the medicine.
They're getting closer.
Help us, Eric.
I need another dose.
Footsteps. Loud, pounding footsteps.
They're not dead.
I need to show them I'm healthy.
You can't be too careful.
They're not dead.
They're not dead.

Dreams

*T*he fires of Hell rose up from the barrels scattered along the alleyways and throughout the city. They illuminated the walls of fallen skyscrapers and pillaged buildings and made the old graffiti red and full:
DIE TYRANT SCUM!
THE REBEL AGE IS HERE!
OUR COUNTRY IS FREE AGAIN!
GOD SMITE THE WICKED!
They illuminated the streets filled with large debris, what couldn't be cleaned up even after two years of peace. And under the black sky, they illuminated two red-clad soldiers dragging their prisoner through what used to be the downtown area. He wore a tattered gray suit, and his head was covered by a burlap sack, even though the whole country knew who he was. He offered little resistance, letting his captors pull him along the barren streets. The man kept his masked head down, and every so often, the soldiers would smirk at each other.

Whatever Rex had done to him, it had been effective.

Other soldiers stopped their patrols and held up their guns as the prisoner passed, but he didn't react. His captors only looked at the other soldiers and nodded to them, telling them to lower their weapons. This man wasn't a fighter. Not anymore.

They passed a few loose posters fluttering in the wind, one of them forced to the ground under a soldier's boot.

Tyrant leader surrenders at Pyrite Amphitheater, it would read if one gave it a passing glance. *September 13th, 2058 at 9:00 pm. The war is over! Rejoice!*

A few blocks away, there was a struggle that ended with several gunshots and scattering pedestrians, some of them covered in blood. Someone had forgotten the rules again, or they thought they could get away with their insolence. Just another night in the Rebel State.

More barrels were lit in the streets as the soldiers and their captive grew closer and closer to Pyrite Amphitheater. They could also hear the rumble of the crowd gathered there, growing louder and louder with every corner they turned, every building they passed. This was the moment they had been waiting for, the moment the remaining Tyrants had put off for two years. Jay Windsor and what was left of his people couldn't ruin it this time.

They entered the old amphitheater, and a thrashing sea of red Rebel uniforms greeted them with jeers and curses. No civilian had stayed home or had more important things to do than witness this historic event; they all knew that after this, the war would officially be over, and they wanted to be there to celebrate.

Waiting for his captive was a man in a plain black suit, standing at center stage behind a lone table and chair. He watched, amused, as the soldiers dragged the prisoner down the aisles toward what was once the orchestra pit.

"I'll take him from here," the man in the black suit said, meeting the soldiers in the front row and grabbing the prisoner by the wrist. The prisoner still didn't fight, which made his new captor smile. As the soldiers headed back to their post, he led the prisoner onto the stage and sat him down in the chair. Suddenly, he pulled the sack off the prisoner's face, revealing his identity to the crowd, who gave a collective and unanimous jeer at the sight of him.

Jay Windsor, the Tyrant leader. The coward who had managed to avoid fighting in his own war and who had evaded capture for so long. Several more soldiers appeared from the back of the stage to keep an eye on Windsor while the man in the black suit raised a hand to quiet the crowd.

"We've come a long way," the man said into the nearby microphone. "No, we *did* it. As of tonight, the old government is gone. We have spoken, we have fought them, and we have won. It took some extra effort since not everyone here was willing to cooperate," he gave a sideways glance at Windsor before looking back at the crowd, "but in the end, we did it. The Tyrants are *gone*. If they're not, they will be soon. And I have you to thank. If it weren't for your support, I'd still be on the streets trying to make a living for myself and my family, trying to survive *their* influence, *their* dominance, *their* intolerance. But now, the tables have turned. Now, we are the ones hunting them, killing them, putting them out of the picture so that we can live the lives we've always dreamed, do the things we couldn't do before, be what we could have been if it hadn't been for them. For the first time in so many years, we will be safe. We will be strong. We will be free. On this momentous occasion, thank you. From the bottom of my heart, thank you, and I hope we can recover from this devastating war."

Throughout the whole speech, Windsor didn't move or speak. He numbly looked down at the document in front of him: the details of his surrender. He just had to sign this and face the humiliation, and then he could—

The crowd roared its approval, and soon a chant rose. It started quietly, indistinguishable, but eventually, it could be heard even over the maniacal cheers: "Rex! Rex! Rex! Rex! Rex!"

Rex grinned at the response. He closed his eyes and took a moment to bask in his praise before speaking again.

"And now, without further ado, the greatest moment in our history."

He turned around and walked back to Windsor, who looked up at Rex upon hearing the end of his speech. Knowing full well that Windsor was watching his every move, Rex pulled a pen out of his coat pocket and handed it to him.

Engraved on it was the name of the last President. Fitting.

As Windsor was about to open the pen, Rex cleared his throat. Windsor looked over, only to find a microphone in his face and Rex's smug expression. Windsor sighed.

"I am a traitor to my country," he muttered, but the

microphone amplified his confession for the whole audience to hear. "On this night, I ... officially declare my surrender and formally disband the P—the Tyrant movement." He hesitated. "It is to the mutual agreement of myself and Rex Libertatis that this civil war should cease immediately." Windsor leaned back in the wooden chair as the crowd roared again. *Now* all he had to do was sign, and it would all be over. He sat up again and took the pen in his hand.

He twisted it open.

He signed his name.

Yes.

Once his full and complete name was on the document, a needle was lodged into the back of Windsor's neck. Rex held the syringe as Windsor froze, wide-eyed.

The world held its breath until Windsor's eyes rolled into his head and he collapsed onto the table.

*

"So, you're the Tyrant leader I've been hearing so much about."

"I am."

Jay—his face a stinging canvas of bruises and crimson streaks, with large rips and gashes in his old best suit from the struggle—sat in near darkness in front of Rex's desk. Between him and the Rebel leader, a small reading lamp flickered, and the end of Rex's cigarette held a constant red glow. Rex took a puff, and as the embers flared, the ornate room was filled with sweet mechanical fumes.

"You look older than I imagined. The war really did a number on you, didn't it? Especially with all the fighting you did."

"Speak for yourself."

Rex's eyes became cold. His expression, bitter. The joviality vanished from his voice as he took another puff, made the embers eat away at the small white stick, and said, "My fighting is done. But let's not talk about me."

He held the cigarette over the ashtray beside him and flicked the ashes into the once spotless bowl. Jay's eyes followed the cigarette, and out of the corner of his eye, he spotted Rex's desk calendar: July 24th. It was the first time that Jay had known today's date in ages.

"Let's talk about you," Rex continued, "and the issue of your surrender."

"Are you going to torture me?" Ever since the war had started, Jay had prepared himself for this moment. If he was captured, forced by the Rebels to back down, he would hold firm to his cause no matter what Rex did to him. He had taught himself to bite back whatever pain he was given, to not show any weakness no matter how much they electrocuted or waterboarded him, or how many hours they sat him in a room alone expecting him to snap. If need be, Jay would become a martyr for his people, an example.

But Rex only chuckled, that boyish charm returning to his face. "I had something a little different in mind. You see, Windsor, I don't believe in hurting people. I did what I did so I could help this country, maybe even the world. It just so happened that certain people were a little defensive about their flawed government system, and if they preferred to be casualties, who was I to stop them? Anyway, like I was saying, I don't believe in hurting people, especially people I respect. The rest of the country wants to see you strapped to a nuclear bomb—you can thank the media for that—but I know you have potential. 'If things had been different' and all that, you know what I mean." He took another puff and tapped the cigarette against the ashtray. "That's why I want to try and help you, too."

Jay felt the hairs stand up on the back of his neck. "No offense, but I think you've helped enough already."

"None taken, and I don't think so because this war is still eating at you. It's been over for two years, and you're acting like it just started yesterday. That's got to be bad for your health, Windsor. And torturing you is only going to make it worse and satisfy your delusions. Hell no, I'm not gonna do that. Anyone else in my position might, but I need to set a good example and show I'm better than that. After all, there's always another solution. A peaceful solution, a *humane* solution to situations like this. It benefits both of us, and it'll help you transition. Cope, even."

"So you're a psychiatrist now."

"I consulted several with the idea I'm about to tell you. They agreed that it was the most efficient way to go about this." Another puff, another tap.

Jay coughed. "What idea?"

"Do you even remember your life before the war?"

Jay did, but he wasn't about to say that to Rex. The war had been an effective distraction from Katharine's death, and there had been times he had almost forgotten about her, almost skipped a day of missing her. There had also been times, though, where Jay wished he had had her support, even in the form of knowing she would still be at their old home when it was all over, and in the form of knowing their lives could go back to normal.

Rex snapped his fingers. "Actually, never mind. I almost forgot. I managed to pull up your files from the public archive, so we can look through all fifty years of your life together. Won't that be fun?"

Rex opened a drawer in his desk and pulled out a folder labeled *WINDSOR, JACOB BERNARD*. He extinguished the cigarette as he opened the folder and methodically spread the papers across his desk. Jay peered over at them as well; his birth certificate, his family history, his work history, hospital record after hospital record, copies of every letter, records of every package he had ever sent or received, copies of his parents' and Katharine's death certificates ... everything that could have been made public about him was all on Rex's desk.

After several minutes of looking through the documents, Rex finally looked up at Jay and smirked.

"That'll work." He gathered all the papers and put them back in the folder.

"Pardon?"

"For my idea. Given your history, you'd be the perfect candidate. You see, I've wanted to test something that's been in development for a while—under my guys, of course. It's been tested in the lab, yeah, so we know it works, but I've always wanted a chance to apply it to the *field*. You know what I mean?

The professionals I consulted, they said it was unconventional, but it could work. They called it ... creative."

Rex reached into another desk drawer and pulled out a small bottle of pills. There was no label, but "Sweet Dreams" was neatly handwritten on the bottle in thick, black permanent marker.

"A drug?"

"Mm-hmm."

"So, what does this have to do with my surrender? I take one of these and the war's over for good?"

Rex chuckled. "Something like that. After you take this, you'll know why all this fighting is useless, and maybe you'll start to see things from my point of view. Maybe the idea of finally ending this war will seem a little more attractive to you."

"And what if I don't take your magic pill? What if I just run?"

Rex narrowed his eyes and sat up in his chair, hunching over the desk. "You wouldn't make it out of this room. The door's locked from the outside, and you wouldn't want to jump out the window once you see how long the fall's going to be. If you attempt to hurt me, I can break both your legs in ten seconds." Without so much as blinking, Rex added, "If you somehow got past me and managed to escape, you still wouldn't get very far. Your respiratory system is weak at best, possibly from a combination of living underground for so long and a certain childhood incident you don't like to talk about. But I digress, if and when the guards catch you, don't expect them to be as polite as I am. Your last moments will be a living Hell, and after that, you die."

Jay leaned back in his chair. "I see your point."

"So, the short answer is: you'll die." Rex sat back as well. "And any reasonable man would want to choose the option that gives him the best chance of surviving. For you, that option is trusting me."

"And if I just sit here? Not taking the pill, not running?"

"Go ahead, filibuster to your heart's content. I have all night. I can keep busy. It'll also give us time to get to know each other. You might starve, but then again, you've gotten quite used to that, haven't you?"

"So I'm assuming my options are limited."

"Right."

Rex was smart, Jay gave him that. He hadn't known what to expect when meeting the man known only as Rex Libertatis for the first time, but his "humane" solution had Jay morbidly curious. Was it really going to "help" him as much as Rex claimed? He did sound genuine in his explanations. There was also the possibility that the drug could be poison, but it was just that: a possibility. Despite Jay's odds, he admitted Rex was right: he needed to choose the outcome that had the better chance of him surviving.

"Alright. I'll do it."

"That's what I like to hear."

Rex stood up and walked to the nearby watercooler, keeping an eye on Jay the whole way there. He filled a small cup before returning to his desk and handing the water to Jay, who nodded his thanks and set the cup down in front of him. Jay unscrewed the lid of the "Sweet Dreams" bottle with some difficulty and poured one of the small tablets into his hand. He hesitated, taking a moment to analyze Rex's expression for any dead giveaways, any signs that Rex had some additional tricks up his sleeve, but there were none. After taking a few more deep breaths, Jay popped the pill into his mouth and drank the whole cup of artificial-tasting water.

He felt nothing at first, but then the world around him distorted and vanished like melted film, the darkness spreading until it enveloped his vision completely.

*

Jay felt as though he had just gotten a good night's sleep, even though he didn't know how long he had been out. He was lying on his back somewhere soft, and part of him began to think that the whole capture had just been a bad dream and that he was really back at the base with Hubert, or maybe even at his old home with Katharine. However, the closer Jay became to consciousness, the more he realized that this felt nothing like any bed he had ever had.

He was lying on grass. The softest, most lush grass he had felt in years.

Jay took several deep breaths. There wasn't a trace of the filthy bunker in the air. There wasn't a trace of anything remotely urban; no smog, no dust and ash, not even Rex's cigarette smoke, the first good smoke he had smelled in years. Everything was pure. When he breathed in, he was welcomed by the scent of fresh dew, and when the wind blew, the wet tips of the thin, spindly grass brushed gently against his skin like tiny paintbrushes, making a masterpiece on the canvas of his scarred and aged face.

No, he wasn't in his bedroom at the base. He wasn't even in the Capital City anymore. Where was he?

He slowly opened his eyes, only to press them shut again. There was a blinding light above him. Light, in the strikingly clear sky. Once his eyes were used to the abundance of color that came with what he faintly remembered as the country sunrise, Jay shakily stood up and looked around, his eyes widening even though they ached from living in darkness for so long.

It was an open field that seemed to go on for miles, life that went on as far as the eye could see. It was strange and yet vaguely familiar. Was this a dream? Jay had never had dreams like this, none that he could remember. It felt so real, but part of him knew it wasn't: the world was so even and balanced, though there were hills and valleys all around him, subtle curves in the ground and steep inclines to the sky.

There was no sound except for the wind rustling the grass and the birds chirping and calling in the distance. Jay took a few steps, and the grass crunched under his charcoal boots in protest of him disturbing the field's serenity.

He needed to know what was going on. He needed answers ...

Jay stopped for a moment before looking up and closing his eyes again. He felt the warmth of the morning sun on his face, unobstructed. It suddenly occurred to him: how long had it been since he had last seen a sunrise? Since he had last *felt* a sunrise? Not since before the war, since he had been too busy saving his own ass during the war and saving others' in its brutal aftermath.

Rex. Jay suddenly remembered what had happened in Rex's office. His capture. Rex's drug. Did it cause all this? Was he hallucinating? If he was, then why did it feel so real?

Jay made his way through the field with more caution. If this was Rex's doing, if he was messing with his head somehow, then Jay needed to fight it. Whatever happened in the dream, he couldn't afford to succumb to any temptations. If Rex managed to weaken his mind, then Jay—and everyone else—would be done for. At least, that's what Hubert had always told him whenever he felt like he was going to snap.

He walked for what felt like several hours, though he wasn't fatigued. Rex was right: Jay's respiratory system was unusually weak, so why wasn't he exhausted? Because it was a dream, he reminded himself. Rex can do whatever he wants.

Up ahead of him, there was a small hill marked by a blot of a tree, a skyscraper compared to the surrounding mob of grass, and a small figure sitting under it. Jay couldn't make out who it was or whether or not they could be trusted, but this was the only other person around for miles. Hopefully, they would have some answers for him.

"Hey!" Jay yelled, his voice rippling through the air. A flock of large birds erupted from the tree and flew in a writhing thundercloud toward the horizon. "Hey! Excuse me!"

As Jay ran up the hill (again, feeling no fatigue), he got a better look at the figure. It was a woman in her mid-thirties wearing a red-and-white sundress that fit her gorgeously. Her brown curls cascaded under the wide brim of her red sunhat, and when she looked up at him, his strength immediately vanished, as did all traces of the dream's lucidity. At the sight of her sweet face, his legs buckled, almost as if his age had finally caught up with him and was punishing his body for its narrow escape.

He knew.

"Katharine?" Jay whispered, looking over every detail, every aspect of her features, making sure it was really her and not some cruel joke ...

"Jay." Katharine's face brightened as she rushed to her feet with the grace of a nymph and embraced him.

He held her as well, tears welling up in his eyes. He had so many questions, but they could wait for now. They could wait.

For a long time, they held each other in silence, afraid that even the slightest sound or movement would tear them apart. He listened to her quiet breathing against his chest and savored it, promising himself never to forget that feeling for the rest of his life. His own breaths were labored, shaky as she pressed her hand just below his shoulder, the struggling staccato of his heart rippling underneath it. The wind brushed past them, fluttering her curls and making his thinning strands quiver.

He buried his face in her hair, his breathing becoming more stable as the sudden rush of lavender healed the damage that time had done to his lungs. Her hair still smelled the same, even after all these years. He had almost forgotten her favorite shampoo. With every breath, more memories came rushing back, memories the war had stolen from him. The wind blew again, forcing the smell through his nostrils and into his lungs, but he didn't mind. He didn't mind at all.

"Where have you been?" he whispered into her ear.

"I've been here all this time, waiting for you."

"Do you mean I'm …? Did I die?"

"No, I don't think so. I'd think you'd know if you did."

Reluctantly, they let go, and Katharine invited Jay to sit down beside her, their backs against the tree. It was then that Jay noticed that Katharine had set up a picnic—blanket, basket, and all.

"How long has it been?" Katharine suddenly asked.

"You don't know?"

"There's not exactly a newspaper here." Her gaze darted from feature to feature of his face. "You look like you've been through Hell."

"I have. You, uh, you missed quite a bit back home."

"Really? Well, tell me all about it."

"Well, that's just it. I, uh … A few years after I lost you, we went to war."

"With who? You didn't have to fight, did you?"

Jay hesitated. "It was a civil war. There was a rebellion, and now the government's destroyed. The Rebels have taken over. A whole bunch of crazy new laws, and if you break even the slightest one, they shoot you on sight. It's a good thing you made me quit smoking when you did."

"They shoot you for smoking?" Katharine was incredulous.

"Tobacco, drugs, alcohol, weapons if you're not a part of the Rebel Army, it's all on the same tier. Making this country a better place to be, they said. And we tried to stop it. We tried to fight back, but they were just too strong. Eventually, we ran out of soldiers and went into hiding before they could force us to surrender. The whole thing was a nightmare. I'm almost glad you weren't there to see it."

"I would have done what I could. Even though I try not to get too involved, I know how much your work meant to you. To see it spiral into something like this …"

"You should hear what the media says about me. About the 'Tyrants.' That's what they call us. We were the Patriots, but they took some … liberties. Made it a little easier for people to understand who the 'good guys' were."

"That's stupid. You can't make politics that clear cut."

"Exactly." Jay sighed, before lying on his back nearby and looking up at the tree. "Because then, something like this happens."

The leaves were summer green, but when the wind blew, they shriveled up, snapped off, and drifted to the ground as if autumn had come when no one was looking. As they fell, they disintegrated into dozens of tiny pink petals each, tossing and turning with the wind as they showered the couple and the world around them.

Katharine laughed as many of the petals hit Jay's face, and Jay found himself laughing, too. Their laughter intermingled, and it echoed through the air, a triumphant fanfare of the first real happiness that Jay had had in years. No, the capture hadn't been a bad dream. The past fifteen years had been a bad dream, and he was only now waking up. He sat up, hair and clothes covered in dots of pink that fluttered to the ground as soon as he moved. Katharine pulled some of the petals out of her hair and tossed them away, sending them to disappear into the void of the wild grass.

"That's why I love this tree," Katharine said. "It does that every once in a while. They all grow back in just a few days. Isn't that amazing?"

"Yeah," Jay replied, settling down from his last fit of laughter. He stopped to think for a few moments before frowning. "Yeah."

"What's wrong?"

"Nothing. It's just that something doesn't feel right. It hasn't felt right since I got here."

"What do you mean? This place is amazing."

"It is, but that's what's bothering me. It's too good."

"'Too good'? Jay, I don't understand. This isn't like you."

"The war taught me to be suspicious, especially of things like this." He paused, the memories of the waking world gradually returning to him. "Before I woke up here, Rex gave me a pill. He said it would help me, get me to see his point of view, make me more willing to surrender. The bottle said 'Sweet Dreams'—I know that's what caused this." He ran his fingers through his hair, only to realize that it had all grown back. However, Jay wasn't concerned about that at the moment. "We have to fight it, Katharine. We can't let him—!" Jay cut himself off, realizing what he had almost said.

"What? Can't let him what?"

" ... Can't let him fool us."

"Look, Jay, I don't know how much time we have together, but I don't want you to waste it thinking about this war. The picnic's still here, we've been waiting for this moment for ... you never told me how long it's been."

Jay sighed. "It's 2058 now. The war started in 2045."

"Wow. It has been a while. But, yeah, Jay, let's forget about that now, please? At least fifteen years ..." Her voice faded as she became transparent, the color draining from her body as she obliviously continued talking.

"Katharine? Katharine!" He jumped to his feet and desperately tried to save her.

She was soundlessly calling him, likely wondering why he was behaving so strangely when she exploded into a storm of petals and drifted away on the wind.

He took off after her before realizing that the world around him was collapsing in the same way. Every hill and valley disintegrated into a whirlwind of petals and enveloped him, overpowered him, pulled the air from his lungs as he watched himself disintegrate ...

*

Jay's eyes snapped open. He took a few deep breaths, only to erupt into a coughing fit. Dust. He was breathing real air again, he knew that much.

And that was when he remembered: he wasn't in the field anymore. It was gone. Katharine was gone. *It had felt so real ...*

Jay struggled to sit up as he looked around. His uncomfortably small and stuffy bedroom in the base hadn't changed much since he had been captured. No light, except for the cheap lantern hanging by the door that flickered longer than stayed lit (the single battery inside was almost dead, he realized, which meant soon, someone would have to go to the surface to snag another one), and no air circulation in the room, save for a perpetual layer of dust hovering above the salvage like a musty hurricane. He lay on his bed, an old, hard mattress in the back of the room facing the metal door. He normally wouldn't have complained about it, but after the dream, his senses had heightened when it came to the various pains in his body. His bones cracked louder than ever before, it hurt for him to breathe, and his joints were tight and stiff.

Suddenly, Jay heard a loud creak that overpowered even that of his aching body. He turned toward its source: an older man in a tattered blue and gold uniform had opened the rusty door and walked into the room, holding a plate of stale biscuits. When Jay realized who it was, he knew this was the man he wanted to see right now.

"Hubert?" Jay asked in between groans.

"Jay." Dr. H. Hubert set the plate of biscuits on the cardboard "nightstand" and sat on the edge of Jay's bed, looking him over for any visible injuries out of force of habit. "Jay, you're alright. I was so worried."

Jay would have normally been embarrassed at Hubert's fussing—he was a grown man, for God's sake!—but now he was relieved that things were back to normal, at least for the time being.

"What happened? How did I get back here? How long—?"

"It's been three weeks. We only managed to rescue you about a week ago, and—you must be starving," Hubert interrupted himself, breaking one of the biscuits in half with a crumbling snap and giving one of the pieces to Jay.

"... I was going to have a picnic."

"What?"

"Nothing. Nothing, it was just a ... dream I had." Jay took a small bite of the biscuit. It didn't make him feel much better, but that was how small rations worked.

"A dream? What kind of dream?" When Jay didn't reply, he repeated, "What kind of dream, Jay?"

Something within him made him tense, similar to how he had felt when he had first met Rex. "I don't remember much of it."

"Cut the crap, Jay." Without giving him a chance to respond, Hubert muttered, "You're captured, you're out for at least a week, and you come back telling me some dream you had." He shook his head. "Nah, nah, he couldn't. He wouldn't sink that low. Or maybe he would since it's Jay." He then spoke up: "I don't think I phrased the question correctly, Jay. Do you remember anything from when you were captured? Did Rex say anything? Do anything? Because if you say you just fell asleep there and didn't wake up for a full week, as far as I know, that is complete and utter bullshit!"

Jay snapped out of his disorientation and managed to overpower his instincts. "He gave me a pill. It was ... 'Sweet Dreams'. That's what it was called."

"God!" Hubert jumped from his seat and started to pace around the room. Despite how much older Hubert was, his body was in miraculously better condition than Jay's, which was why Jay assumed he had led the rescue. "God, Jay, why did you take it? If you knew what it was—oh, *God*, this was my fault. It's my fault. I knew I should have told you. I should have prepared you. I didn't know he was going to pull something like this, and why didn't I? He knew we wouldn't have seen it coming! Aah!" He ran his fingers through his full head of wiry white hair, almost pulling clumps out of his scalp.

"What—you knew about it this whole time?" Jay tried to sit up, but Hubert rushed back to his bedside to stop him. "And for your information, I had no choice. If I didn't take it, I wouldn't have gotten out of there alive. So don't talk to me like I'm an idiot, Hubert! I'm not a child!"

Hubert sighed in defeat. "You're right. I'm sorry. I suppose I underestimated him and how he probably planned this all out. And, yes, I did know about it. I should have told you sooner, but there's no time like the present, as they say. Several months ago," he explained, "some of the tech guys and I intercepted some partial development plans for a project Rex was personally funding. It was a new drug called *perpesomnagalantamine*, but the codename was 'Sweet Dreams'. It was intended to be some sort of pleasure drug, probably to keep the middle and lower classes under control so they wouldn't start thinking all of a sudden. We didn't get the full details, but it was insignificant at the time, and I didn't want to bother you about it. You had more important things to lose sleep about, and at the time, you were so wound up you were on the threshold of making some *risky* decisions."

Jay scowled. "Stupid decisions."

"If you don't like my euphemism, then fine. Your sense of judgment was cloudy at best under as much pressure as you were—and on the run from the law, to boot—so I thought it best to sweep it under the rug. You'd eventually find out on your own, but," Hubert sighed, "I never thought it would be like this."

"You should have told me anyway."

"And what?!" Hubert jumped to his feet once more, this time nearly stumbling. "Given you a damn stroke because you'd never take your medications again? You'd never sleep again, either! And for what, a damn pleasure-pill? You're paranoid enough for my liking, boy! What'd you want me to do, make it worse?" His booming voice echoed through the small bunker. Realizing his volume, Hubert took a few breaths and settled down. "But I suppose it doesn't make a difference now. He made you take it. He threatened you. He ... He'd turned it into a weapon. If I'd'a known that then, I would have told you even if you did have a stroke over it. It would have been a legitimate threat, but I didn't think of it. I feel horrible, Jay, I ... Now I know what your headaches feel like." He leaned against the wall, pressing his fingertips to his temples while still looking in Jay's direction.

"It's fine, Hubert, but with all due respect, try to keep from doing it again in the future. We can't afford to make mistakes, not when we're planning to ..." He trailed off, the conviction draining from his voice.

"Now, boy, you should know better than to—!" Hubert started his usual response for whenever Jay overstepped his boundaries, but he soon noticed the anomaly in Jay's command. "What's wrong?"

Jay hesitated for several moments, before: "I saw Katharine again."

"He made you see Katharine. Oh, Jay—"

"She was exactly as I remember her. *Exactly* as I remember her, but she was healthy. She didn't look—she looked just as beautiful as on the day we met. You should have seen her, Hubert. She wore her favorite dress—the one I got her for her birthday—the matching hat, and by God, Hubert, I never thought I would smell that shampoo again in my life." He was barely able to form the words as he burst into tears. "And we still didn't ... We still didn't have that picnic. She'd set it up and everything, all ready to go, but I just couldn't ... I wanted to, but ... I was worrying too much, and ... I have to go back."

"Jay—"

"Hubert, I have to. I only have one chance to do this, I need to—"

"Jay, it wasn't real. She's not real."

"She was!"

"Jay, it's not her! Don't you dare—!" Hubert cut himself off, his eyes widening. He jumped out of his seat for a third time before frantically pacing around the room. "Oh, my God. Oh, my God, it all makes sense now. It all makes sense. Why didn't I see this before? It all makes sense now."

"What do you mean?"

"Why the rescue was a success, and ... and why we're the only ones who got out."

Jay froze. The room was silent. He tried to process this

information before asking, "E-everyone else?"

"Dead, probably. Dead, or being tortured. It's just us now, kiddo. Just the two of us."

Jay sank into the mattress. The small remaining group of Patriot supporters, the ones who had been too old or sick to fight in the war... dead, except for him and Hubert. He stared blankly at the flickering lantern by the door. There was no one left to send to the surface to get supplies. No one to intercept transmissions, no one to watch for Rebel soldiers (not that anyone needed to anymore). No one to chat with, no one to talk him through any of his nervous breakdowns. Except for Hubert. The two of them, together, as it had always been, but even they wouldn't be able to carry the Patriot movement on their own.

"And he *let* us get away, that's the thing," Hubert continued. "He *let* us. He let you get away just to see you crawl right back to him. And he *knew* it would work. He was so confident that—I can't believe this. Here, I thought I still had it in me," he muttered to himself before continuing, "You better not go back there, I'm telling you right now. If you're not going to listen to me as a comrade, you better listen to me as a father because I'm telling you right now, it's not real. She's not really there. She doesn't give two shits about your damn picnic. He's just trying to get to you, and she's the one who makes you roll on your back and cry uncle. Oh, hell, I forgot—biscuits are still here if you want any more." He noticed Jay's blank stare and softened his voice. "I know this is a lot to take in, Jay, but try to get some rest. That's your first priority right now. You need time to get your strength back because you need it. Once you're feeling better, we'll talk about what we're going to do next, but for now, get some sleep. Some *actual* sleep, if you don't mind."

"Alright."

Hubert started toward the door, but then he looked over his shoulder. "And Jay?"

"Yeah?"

"When I say don't go back to Rex, I mean it. I mean it more than anything I've ever said. I know you miss her, Jay. I know you think you owe her. I know you think you saw her again, but you need to realize it's a trap. Going back there just means he'll win, and it also means I'll lose you. And if I lose you, I won't be able to live with myself. But don't worry about that now. Get some rest."

"Where are you going?"

"Up to the surface. I guess it's a good thing everyone else is dead because ... well, larger rations, whether we like it or not. Like I said, get some rest. I'll see you when I get back."

Hubert left, shutting the metal door behind him, and as he took another nibble of a stale biscuit, Jay could hear panging footsteps fade into the distance. He closed his eyes and could hear the clanks, rattles, and booms of the bunker door being opened, closed, and locked from the outside. There was silence after that, and Jay fell asleep.

*

Hubert made Jay spend the next week in bed. Jay initially objected, but the older man was surprisingly capable of running the base on his own, mainly because there wasn't much to do anymore. Although Rex and the Rebel soldiers now knew their location, there hadn't been any threats or even patrols in the area since Jay's capture. They were keeping their distance, eager to see what Rex's little lab rat would do next.

Rex's little lab rat lay awake on his cold, hard mattress, his eyes never leaving the cloud of dust swirling just below the ceiling. Sleep always evaded him because every time he closed his eyes, he could hear *her* calling him, asking where he was, begging him to help her finish what they had started. He could hear her as though she was just above ground or a few hollow rooms away.

He needed to go back. There was just no way around it. He didn't care if she wasn't real. They had both been planning this afternoon for such a long time, and when they finally had the opportunity, he'd been the one to waste it. And doing what? Worrying. Being concerned that this was all a part of Rex's grand plan. And it had been, that was the thing. It *had* been.

He remembered when Katharine was feeling well, when he couldn't spend much time with her because that election year, his competition for the Senate seat had been deadly. By the time he had secured his place, Katharine's health started to decline. It steadily became worse and worse before one day, he had come home from work and found her sitting on the couch, looking out the window. That was when she told him that she had gone to see the doctor, and he told her that she had lung cancer because Jay always forgot to open the windows when he smoked. He was devastated, but she insisted that it wouldn't stop them from taking a weekend, maybe a Sunday afternoon, to go to the park and have a picnic like they originally planned. He promised her that he would get some time off, but by the time he did, it was too late.

She was probably still sitting under that tree, wondering what had happened to him. The picnic was still there, untouched. Luckily, in a place like that, the food would last a while, maybe forever. But he needed to go back at some point. He couldn't just leave her. Not again.

Suddenly, she was almost skeletal, the sundress loosely draped over her frail body. Her glassy eyes bulged and she could barely breathe as the wind yanked out clumps of her hair and sent them sailing toward the bright red horizon. Bright red? But it was sunrise. Or was it sunset?

Katharine was trying to talk to him, but Jay could only hear scratchy gurgling from her throat as crimson rose petals fell endlessly from her mouth and drifted to the ground in front of them. As she reached a bony hand toward him, the tree caught fire and the wind scattered its embers into the sky, where they fell like petals once again and ignited the grass and ate away—

Jay's eyes snapped open. He hadn't realized he had fallen asleep. His gasps echoed throughout the empty room as he tried to ground himself in reality once again.

Reality. He wasn't in the field anymore. He never had been. He was back at the base with Hubert, who was probably sleeping now as well. When Jay felt better and was able to think clearly again, they would work out a plan for how to retaliate, or at least how to carry on. If they played their cards right, they would be able to get more resources, maybe even recruit. Rebuild the Patriot movement, try once more to take back what was theirs. All they needed was time and patience, that was all. Time and patience, and they would be able to get right back to work.

Work. Jay closed his eyes and let another memory haunt him: a haphazard Patriot rebellion, peacefully protesting and defending the Capitol from a group of Rebel soldiers. It was early in the war, back when the Rebels' ideas were still seen as "radical" and the government still had substantial support from the people. Jay had watched helplessly from the shadows as the soldiers opened fire and these young men and women were turned to bloody slush right before his eyes.

Those innocent faces—blood-covered, terrified, confused, mid-sob, twisted in pain right before the light had left their eyes for good—had haunted him for years. Glassy brown eyes, a blue eye and a half, no eyes at all looking straight at him. That was what he had always seen whenever he closed his eyes before. This twisted form of withdrawal had been a welcome change.

But Jay reminded himself that those faces had haunted him for a reason. They were innocent people who had given their lives to his cause—to *his* cause—and he needed to avenge them. Many of his soldiers, the ones who didn't immediately convert to the Rebels' side, had probably died like this, too. The same for his few remaining comrades who had joined Hubert on the rescue mission—the mission to get *him* out of the Rebel base—and never came out. He couldn't let those sacrifices—the lives that were given so that *he* could keep fighting—go to waste. That would be exactly what Rex wanted him to do, to show that he was blind and selfish, that he could be broken. No, he couldn't afford to do that. He couldn't afford to give Rex that satisfaction, that *pleasure* in knowing that Jay Windsor had been defeated by his own greed.

Was it greed, though?

He could hear her calling him again.

Was it greed?

A better question was: was it worth it?

Jay didn't have an answer for that yet, no matter how many times he asked himself. He knew what Hubert had said, and he knew what Katharine would say, and part of him knew what *Katharine* would have said. He knew what Rex would say as well, but would he believe him? Would Jay allow himself to believe him? After all, Rex's morals and ideals were incredibly corrupt, and his version of "help" would do nothing but destroy him. But would it really? What if he was right, just this once? What if Rex really was genuinely concerned about him, and his words weren't just hollow and artificial? No, he was never "genuine." He always had an ulterior motive—that's what gets a man anywhere in this business, after all. Rex's was to make him surrender, to end the war once and for all by making him admit the Patriots didn't have a chance at coming back. He knew that for a fact, but did it change anything?

Jay knew that resisting Rex was what was best for the Patriot movement, but what was best for himself? What would happen if he surrendered? What would happen if he didn't? If he didn't, he knew in his gut that nothing would change until he or Hubert died. The stress would probably kill them both eventually.

And if he surrendered?

It would be better for him, he realized. Better for him than the war, better for him than the old metal bunker they called home, better for him than *living*. Eventually, he would suffocate, asphyxiate here with all the dust above him and the smoke and the smog in the air outside, regardless of what he did or what happened to him. It was only a matter of where he wanted his mind to be when that happened.

No, he couldn't afford to think like that, not now. They just needed time.

But how much time?

Time neither of them had.

And, meanwhile, all the time in the world with Katharine. A picnic every day for the rest of their lives, if he wanted to, but only if he was there. If he died, there was no guarantee he would ever see Katharine again. But if he took Rex's unspoken deal now, if he *willingly* took more of the Sweet Dreams? There would be. There would be an absolute, irreversible guarantee that he would see Katharine, and they would be able to live as if the war had never happened.

But she's not real.

Hubert wouldn't have said that if he had seen her. If he had been there.

But he hadn't. That's why he saw it for what it was.

At this point, Jay didn't care what it was or what it really was. It was what he needed right now.

*

"It helped you, didn't it?"
"It did."
"Honestly, it's a miracle. Impressive half-life, too. I was expecting you to be out maybe ... a few days at most, but *three weeks*! It's a major setback, but holy shit! I'll have to give those guys a raise. Anyway, back to business."

Jay sat in Rex's office again, and he couldn't help but notice that the younger man was in a much better mood than before, which was certainly saying something given how smug Rex had been right after Jay's capture.

"So you want me to give you another one of these." Rex held up the bottle of pills, his fingers barely covering the handwritten "Sweet Dreams" label.

"Yes." Jay had to force the word out of his mouth, but it was all he could say.

"Thing is, though, it's not like the last one. Consider that one a freebie. All you had to do was agree not to kill yourself. For this one, I want a little bit more than that."

"My surrender."

"At the Pyrite Amphitheater. You remember where that is?"

Jay scowled. "Barely. Why there?"

"The people will want to see it, of course. And, you know, I must listen to the people." Rex grinned, and Jay wanted nothing more than to knock all his teeth out. However, he knew his place, at least for now. "You take this now, and when you wake up, all you have to do is face a little public humiliation. Then, you can go back to the dream and stay there."

Jay paled, his anger vanishing quicker than it had come. "Permanently?"

"Exactly. Based on the data we gathered from your last 'visit', we'll come up with something you'll like."

Jay tried to push back his doubts, tried to remind himself that this was what was best for *him* at the moment, tried to tell himself it was too late to resist. It was too late to go back.

Still, that didn't stop him from imagining Hubert bursting into the room just before Jay took the pill, pleading for him to stop, to go back.

But it was too late. It had always been too late.

*

The worries of the real world faded from his mind as he once more inhaled the scent of fresh dew and felt the gentle breeze coax the tall grass against his skin. He couldn't open his eyes, not yet; he knew they would need time to adjust to the brightness of the sky above him. For now, Jay took in every small sensation of lying in the grass, breathing in the fresh country air, and he wondered why he had ever wanted to leave. He wondered why he had ever prevented himself from coming back here, why he had ever resisted. This was where he needed to be. This was where he felt truly happy.

The scent of lavender drifted on the wind, and it encouraged him to chance opening his eyes. When he sat up, Jay noticed Katharine sitting on a large rock several feet away.

"Katharine!" He jumped to his feet and rushed over to her.

Katharine turned to face him, and her eyes lit up.

"You came back." She looked healthy again, exactly the same as when he had taken the pill before. Jay had to remind himself that the dreams he had had during his recovery weren't real. His own mind had manufactured them, and ...

If those were manufactured, then what was this?

"I did." He grinned as he examined her face once again, trying to convince himself it was really her. However, his grin faded. "But where's the tree? Where's—?"

"The picnic? I figured that could wait for a while longer. After all, you only have so much time here, so I figured I'd show you as much as possible." Katharine jumped to her feet as well, before smoothing the wrinkles in her sundress.

"I'm sorry about that," he blurted out.

"It's fine. I guess I shouldn't have expected you to stay here for very long. After all, you have work."

His heart sank when she said that, but he knew it was true. Even though he didn't have work as she knew it anymore. Even though he was truly happy. He was happy here. This was where he felt happy.

"Not to mention I have something else to show you," Katharine added. She started to walk toward the horizon, and her dress fluttered as the wind blew. "This way."

They walked together through miles of field, up and down small hills and slopes, and Jay never felt fatigued. Just like last time, it felt as though he had walked for hours, but not once had he *felt* it. Time passed, but the color of the sky never changed. The sun stayed in its modest place at the edge of the horizon. Time passed, and yet time stood still.

A while later, something clicked in Jay's mind. "This looks familiar."

Katharine looked over her shoulder. "Familiar?"

"I don't know, it just feels like I've been here before. I've definitely never been here before, but … I mean, it can't be where I first woke up, and I highly doubt we've been walking in—"

Jay cut himself off as they reached the top of a tall hill overlooking the sea of grass below, and in that sea of grass was the only manmade structure in the entire field: a small farmhouse with a thin gravel driveway that stretched across the plain into oblivion. Suddenly, everything made sense: the field, the plain, the sun, the farmhouse, the … the faint scent of smoke lingering in the air. Or was that just his imagination?

"Jay, what's wrong?"

"Katharine, I … I remember this place."

"Remember it? I was just going to show it to you because—"

"Katharine, I've been here. This was … I grew up here. Well, to an extent."

"Wow. Jay, I … I'm sorry, I didn't know it would trigger—"

"No, no, it's fine. It's just … Are they still here?"

"Who?"

Jay turned to look at her. "My parents."

The house was falling apart all around him. There was fire everywhere, and it hurt. He couldn't breathe. He wanted to run, but where were Mama and Papa? He needed them. He needed them now more than ever.

"Jay!"

Mama couldn't breathe, either. He wanted to go to her, he wanted to stay with her because he was scared, but she kept yelling at him, telling him to leave. Leave? But that meant he would be by himself. He wanted to say something to her, but he couldn't speak. He was afraid, and he had breathed in too much of the black stuff—smoke. He could only cough, and so could Mama, but that didn't stop her from telling him to run.

He heard a noise from above and jumped out of the way, curling up into a ball. A big piece of the house had fallen between him and Mama, and a big, menacing wall of fire was keeping him from seeing her. He heard Mama yelling, screaming his name ... and then nothing. Just the fire making its noise and hurting him and keeping him from breathing ...

"Jay!"

He barely heard footsteps, someone running toward him. The voice was familiar, but he couldn't remember who it was right away. He was being picked up and carried outside. He could never remember what happened after that, but he eventually got better, even though he would have trouble breathing for the rest of his life ...

"Hubert saved me that day," Jay mumbled, beginning to regret going back to Rex when Katharine put her hand on his shoulder.

"I'm sorry. You never did tell me—"

"It's fine. Let's go in."

They made their way down the hill and toward the farmhouse. Hubert had always told him stories about his parents, what kind of people they were and what the farm had been like before it burned down. No one ever figured out what had started the fire that night, but it was a miracle that Jay had survived.

Jay and Katharine stood on the rickety front porch. It didn't look like it could hold the weight of two grown adults, but with the way this dream worked, Jay supposed, anything was possible. He tried the rusty old screen door, and it swung open, although Jay had to balance it to keep it on its hinges.

The inside of the old house was the only part of the field that wasn't alive and vibrant with color. The whole interior was a mix of bland pastels: off-white wallpaper patterned with faded flowers and an uneven dark-beige wood floor. The city man towered over nearly everything in the farmhouse, including the blandly dressed man and woman sitting at the old dinner table. The man and woman he faintly, faintly remembered.

He didn't need to say anything. Although they were surprised to see him at first, they welcomed him with their eyes and invited him to sit at the table. There was an empty chair across from them, just for him. Katharine stepped back toward the wall as Jay tentatively approached the chair and sat down. He looked at his feet, and then up at his parents. His parents, who hadn't aged since the farm burned down, who were living images from his lost childhood, the missing pieces from his memory. Every time he looked up at them, his vision began to blur, and he knew it wasn't from the bright sunlit sky outside. Tears fell down his cheeks, the city man looking upon the simple people, and he felt a gentle touch on his forearm that sent chills running through his body. Jay looked over and saw his mother looking at him with gray eyes, her thin, gray-streaked brown hair framing her face.

She said something, and it took a moment for him to process the fact that she was only mouthing words. No sound was coming out. He was about to say something when he heard the rustle of the wind and fluttering petals in the distance. He paled. *No ...*

Katharine was saying something, too, and then they were all saying things to him, but the rustling grew louder. His surroundings slowly disintegrated into a storm of pink petals.

No! Please, not now!

He tried to fight back, struggled more than he had last time, but the more he fought, the quicker the air was pulled out of his lungs by the dream's cruel magic, and everything around him vanished once again as he was carried far, far, further away ...

*

A lethal injection. That's what Rex had said. Although he

wouldn't die, it was very likely he wouldn't wake up.

As Jay signed his name on the declaration of surrender, a cloud of voices materialized in his mind. He heard Hubert pushing for him to resist, begging him, saying that it wasn't too late. He heard Katharine and his parents, calling him from the other side. He heard the unanimous cry of the unavenged souls who had died for a lost cause. But Jay didn't care anymore. He didn't care about anything anymore. Each drop of ink that collectively formed his signature gradually numbed his mind to the outside world before the needle even touched his skin.

The roars of the crowd abruptly dissolved as he felt the pinprick in the back of his neck, and he felt the drug course through his system, numbing his whole body one square inch at a time.

Each breath took an hour. Each blink, ten minutes. But his mind had accelerated, getting his last conscious thoughts out of the way before the drug conquered all.

Every exhale was a gust of wind that caressed the wild grass. The spotlights of the amphitheater stage were all suns, overpowering even the smog-filled sky. This was it. He was going back.

He would never abandon Katharine again. He would never lose his family again. He would be *free*. All he had to do was wait a few more moments, and then he could fall asleep.

Jay took a few more deep breaths, savoring the smog-filled air and letting it have one last strike against his lungs before his eyes rolled back into his head and he barely felt the impact of his limp body striking the table.

And then
he slept.

The Judgment Day to Come

On this clear night, the desert was silent. Only one manmade structure rose above the endless expanse: a small inn, haphazardly made, on the far outskirts of town. Ezra Collinsworth sat on a rocking chair on the porch and looked up at the holy canvas of stars before him, the moon slowly shifting in the sky. The old man rocked back and forth, the slow, quiet creaks of wood on wood keeping time as the wind occasionally passed through or coyotes cried in the distance. For a while, there was no other sound.

But as the moon burned bright red, Ezra thought he heard something in the distance. It was a murmur at first, but as it grew closer, Ezra could tell that it was a man singing, a haunting voice that carried on the dry wind. The discordant twang of an old guitar, too, could now be heard, plucking out some odd melody the old man couldn't place.

The silhouette of a horse and rider gradually rose from the starlit horizon as the words of the song grew clear:

> "Fires burn, and waters flow
> 'Cross the barren earth, he go
> Th' endless sleep he'll never know
> Till the judgment day do come."

Ezra eyed the singing man carefully as he stopped his horse in front of the porch but did not dismount.

"Evenin', Mister." What else could he say?

The rider replied with a quiet, "Evenin'," and tipped his hat, covering his eyes with the brim. But in a way the old man couldn't explain, he could *feel* the rider's eyes on him, sizing him up almost curiously, giving him chills and making his hair stand on end. The rider didn't have the look of a bandit, none Ezra had ever known, but there was still something quite unnerving about him.

"A bit late to be out travelin'," Ezra said, a little wary. "Course, there are worse places to be. Much worse."

The rider nodded slowly. "I've been through worse places, yes."

"You been on the trail long?"

"Long time."

"If you don't mind my askin', where you from? Ain't seen the likes of you 'round here before."

The man remained stoic. He hardly flinched or even raised his tone as he replied, "Does it matter?"

Ezra was taken aback. "I guess it don't. You lookin' to stay the night?"

"Yes, sir." There was a ghost of a smile on the rider's face as he finally dismounted, guitar still in hand, and hitched his horse. He walked up the porch steps and leaned against the old support beam, standing about five feet away from the old man's rocking chair, allowing Ezra to get a better look at him. His dark hair and beard were wild and unkempt as if he'd spent his whole life out in the desert oblivion. However, his eyes were a bright, almost polished silver, as if he'd stolen the moon's pure light and held it for ransom in his soul. The blacks of his pupils stood out like two lumps of coal in fresh mountain snow.

"You got a name?"

Again, the rider hardly reacted. "I don't."

"You don't?" Ezra snapped out of a brief trance that he didn't know he'd been in. He knew this was the strangest man he'd ever seen, just from the rider's looks alone, but the sudden confirmation of the fact baffled him. The man could have simply refused to say anything, or at least given him a fake name to mislead anyone on his trail, but to just say he didn't *have* a name? "Now, look, Mister, if you're plannin' to stay here, I've got to know your name, at least! I have the right to know just who's usin' my facility, after all. Not to mention I need someone to call for breakfast in the mornin'."

The rider remained unfazed. "Mighty kind to offer, but I doubt I'd stay for breakfast. Not to refuse your hospitality, kind sir, but I'm just not the type to take more'n what I need from a gen'rous man. Best save your food for someone who needs it more'n me."

"Now, I insist! If you're a well-meanin' man, I can't see why you shouldn't have a bite to eat while you stay." Was he a well-meaning man? Ezra couldn't tell. The man was odd, but Ezra knew that sometimes, "odd" was harmless. "Odd" was a group of drunks performing a spectacle, the town lunatic spouting nonsense, a man passing through town without a hand, leg, or eye. This man was downright unsettling. Ezra visibly tensed as he continued, "You may as well—no extra charge, and it ain't as if there's a famine right now. If I run out, I can always tell Dirk to go to town and get more. That ain't the problem if there is one."

"All I want's a few hours rest, and I'll be gone before you know it. No use worryin' 'bout me when there's other folks stayin' here. If you say I can have what I want, then that's what I want. No more'n that."

The old man hesitated. Whether it was for several moments or several minutes, he had no way of knowing.

"Now, what's your name?" he asked again, all ability to think of other questions having left him.

The silver-eyed rider sighed. "If you insist on callin' me somethin', then I guess you can call me Stranger. I'll answer to that. Or Mister, or anythin' else you can think of."

"Very well, Stranger." Part of him still couldn't believe this was happening—a disturbance in the tranquil night, a ripple in the stagnant country. "You can pay me now, we'll go in and I can show you up to your bed, or—"

"If it's no trouble, you think we can stay out here a while longer? Best time of the night, and I'd sure enjoy the comp'ny after a long day." He almost broke his monotone and appeared completely content, almost euphoric when he glanced over at the old man. He frowned. "I know that look."

"Pardon?"

"Y'think I'm gonna shoot you or somethin'. I see why you'd think that. Perfect time and place to off ya. Middle of the night, a ways away from town. Aside from the couple o'folks in that inn, we're all alone. Those folks would start talkin', of course, and then I'd have to shoot them, too, I guess, so that word don't get out. No witnesses. You know the rest." Stranger placed his guitar on the top step of the porch and raised his arms over his head as he stood up straight. "I ain't got no weapons. No guns, knives, nothin' on me. Now, I know you don't believe me, so you can check my pockets, my bag, my horse, check my boots if it pleases you. It'll only support the fact that I didn't take nothin' with me when I left, and I don't got nothin' now. Just this here guitar, and I'd rather keep it safe than snap it over a man's head just b'cause he looked at me funny. I think you'd understand when I say I wouldn't do somethin' like that to my prized possession."

"Suppose so."

"I ain't here to cause trouble, and I sincerely wish you'd believe me when I say it. I'd just appreciate the comp'ny. That's all. If I ever lay a hand on you, then God smite me."

Ezra could tell that Stranger genuinely wanted to be trusted. This wasn't the face of a con artist or a murderer, but a man who was more often accused of being one. However, his promise also sounded rehearsed, as if he had said this to many people in many places, perhaps whenever he wanted shelter or rest. This didn't reassure him at all; if Stranger was so desperate to be trusted by his fellow men, what'd he do to lose their trust in the first place?

"Alright, comp'ny it is. Have a seat, Stranger."

Nodding his thanks, Stranger slowly, carefully bent down to pick up his guitar, his silver gaze never leaving the old man as, with guitar in hand, he approached and sat down in the empty rocking chair beside him. As soon as he collapsed into the chair, a burst of a sigh left Stranger's mouth as if the man had just had the wind knocked out of him. When he saw the old man staring at him, Stranger sat up and cleared his throat.

"I'll pay ya now." Before Ezra could comment, Stranger pulled a small bag out of his coat pocket and handed it to the old man.

"That's for the night, and a little extra for your kindness."

The old man looked inside the bag. Gold! Forty antique-looking coins, at least. If he had to guess, this small bag was worth more than Ezra had made in his entire life. About *twice* as much. Suddenly, his fear returned: Where had Stranger gotten all this gold? Was he a thief? Had he found it somewhere? Had he mined it himself? More importantly, why'd he give it to an old man in a shabby inn if he could afford to buy out the whole state? Did Stranger need to get rid of it for some reason? Was he trying to hide something?

"Y-You didn't ha—"

"Goodwill, Mister. Goodwill."

"But ... but it's *gold*!"

"So's an old man's kindness to his fellow man in need," Stranger replied, absently strumming that old guitar, "in need of a quiet porch where he can sit and think about his life, where he's gonna go from here. Beautiful night, ain't it?" He stopped playing and took off his hat, setting it on the ground beside him. The lack of a shadowy brim over those silver eyes, which now glowed their brightest, filled them with even more sincerity. "I don't blame ya for sittin' out here this late. The universe is dancin' in God's great theater, and you've got Earth's best seat."

Ezra said nothing. He only looked out into the distance, affirming what Stranger had said. The moon was still red, although its bright hue was beginning to fade. The stars—the whole infinity of them—twinkled and shone, tiny glints of light in Stranger's eyes. The world was silent, aside from the distant howl of wind and the hypnotic off-key tune that Stranger resumed plucking on that old guitar. Coyotes cried every so often, sometimes nearby, sometimes far away. It was, indeed, a theater where the universe danced.

"That tune you're playin'," Ezra asked some time later, "which one is that? I've never heard it before."

"I figured you wouldn't," Stranger replied. "It's a little song I wrote while I was travelin'. I sing it whenever the trail gets too lonely for me. Makes me feel better, makes it seem like things are gonna change. Like for once, somethin' good's gonna happen. Ya know what I mean?"

"I do. It's a beautiful song, from what I've heard of it."

"Thank you," Stranger replied. "I'll let ya hear more if you like."

"I wouldn't mind it, no," Ezra replied. There was still the nagging fear, of course, that Stranger was only putting on a show to catch the old man unaware when he would kill him, but Ezra was still fascinated by that old guitar, curious about what exactly that decrepit instrument could do.

Smiling, Stranger strummed a few more chords and began again:

> "Desert gold and ocean blue,
> Forest green, and meadow, too
> Still no sign o' the golden hue
> Of the judgment day to come.
>
> 'We've walked this earth, my horse and I
> We've seen the years go sailin' by
> I long for rest, though I've nowhere to lay
> So on we go, without a friend
> For mine's a pain that none can mend
> It's a lonely road towards the judgment day.'"

Stranger hummed the odd melody for a while, absorbed in the world of his song, before looking over at the spellbound old man.

"I thank you for lettin' me join ya out here tonight," Stranger said, standing up to go inside.

"It's no trouble," Ezra breathed. "Now, you go inside and take a nice, long rest."

Stranger nodded, and as he turned around to go inside, Ezra could have sworn he saw a smirk on the other man's face. Then again, it could have also been the shadows playing tricks on him ...

"You, too, Ezra Collinsworth."

*

The next morning, Ezra Collinsworth was dead.

When Stranger was confronted in his room at the inn, he hardly reacted to the news. He only sat on the small bed, absently strumming that old guitar. It was almost as if he had expected this to happen.

"I'm just gonna let you people believe what you want," Stranger would say to those who asked him, "'cause nothin' I say's gonna change your mind."

The only person who didn't bombard Mr. Stranger with questions and accusations was a fair young man not much older than fifteen. He came in and greeted Stranger, who nodded a greeting back.

"I guess you're tired of people askin' ya."

"Nothin' new," Stranger was focused on the strings of the old guitar, plucking them individually and strumming a few experimental chords. "Never gets better, though. I suppose you've come to ask me, too?"

"Not as rudely."

This made Stranger chuckle and look up at him, leaving the guitar alone. There was a strange gleam in those silver eyes, still reflecting the stars from the previous night. "I appreciate that."

"Though I was close to the man who died this mornin', I respect the Good Lord's message. I'd be wise to treat you just as I'd treat anyone else."

Stranger smirked. "A good way to not be on the bad side of a murderin' man, whether the Good Lord's involved or not."

"Are you a murderin' man?" the boy asked. "It don't matter to me. I'd pray for ya either way, you know."

"I appreciate your tryin'," Stranger replied. "And who might you be, other than an angel of the Lord?"

"Dirk, sir. Dirk Collinsworth. Ezra was my granddad. We've been workin' together a long time."

"How long?"

"Ever since my dad died," Dirk replied. "I helped Granddad start the inn, and I've been helpin' run it, too. Been runnin' it for as long as I could work."

"And where were you when I came to visit?"

"In the next town over, gettin' firewood. Granddad said he

could run the inn by himself, so I thought it was gonna be alright to leave him alone. When I got back this mornin', they told me he was gone, and it looked like you were the one that done it."

"Does it?"

"Well, no blood, so I can't see how you would've shot or stabbed him. He didn't look in pain, either, I don't think. Still, they say you were the last one who talked to him, and, well, you're the only one they don't know anythin' about, so they think you must've done somethin' somehow. So, did you? You ca—"

"I can tell you, yes. I know." Stranger thought it over for a few moments, before picking at the guitar again with his gnarled fingers. "T'honest truth, now, that's a little complicated. Can't explain it, simply 'cause you don't want an explanation, you want a simple 'yes' or 'no' to get the hangin' over with, and that's an answer I'm afraid I can't give. I'll just say this, though: I was at a bad place at a bad time."

"So you didn't kill him."

"I never said that."

Dirk frowned. "Then what are you sayin'?"

"I'm sayin' what I said. Bad place at a bad time." He plucked a sour note, which pulled him back to reality. He looked back up at Dirk. "There's no 'yes' or 'no' in that."

"What did you say your name was?"

"I didn't."

"What is it, then?"

Stranger chuckled. "Boy, you ask a lot of questions." He started to strum the guitar again, picking up where he left off. "Like I told your granddad before he died, I don't have a name."

"Then what do folks call you?"

"Besides you and your granddad, folks don't call me nothin'. They don't bother."

"And why's that?"

"Again, that's a little complicated, and it'd be better if I didn't try to explain. I will say, though, that if I had one, I long since forgot it. 'Sir' or 'Mister' lasted me this long, so I'd suggest those, or the name I suggested to your granddad last night, the name 'Stranger.'"

"Stranger." Dirk reflected on this for a few moments. "Sounds like an awful shady name."

There was a twinkle of mischief in Stranger's moonlight eyes. "Well, to most people, I'm an awful shady guy."

*

No one knew when, why, or to whom Stranger had finally confessed, but he had been very nonchalant about it as if murder was only a mundane matter. It had been reported as something along the lines of, "If it satisfies you," and nothing more. He did not "break," as everyone had expected him to do; he did not cry out in anguish and guilt from the pressure the whole town was putting on him, yet the mere fact that he had confessed so casually only made the townsfolk more convinced that he was guilty of his crime. Therefore, the mysterious Stranger, the man who had come into town on the night of the red moon, was set to be hung the next day.

Stranger sat in his small, dark jail cell, absently strumming the old guitar just as he had done when he had first been confronted, just as he had done the night he had met the old man. He didn't look worried or vengeful but weary as if he had been condemned to death many times before and was now bored of it.

The only man who stopped in to see him and didn't jeer or shudder at his gaze was the Lord's messenger, that young man Dirk. He sat across from the condemned man and observed every one of his features, his expressions, every minute reaction to everything that happened around him, but especially those eyes, still glowing in the darkness, that told so much and so little at the same time.

"You're not afraid," Dirk observed. "You're not concerned about bein' hanged?"

Stranger, looking up from his guitar and scrutinizing the boy through the bars of his cell, gave a short, breathy chuckle. "Why should I be?"

"What about death? You 'fraid of death?"

"Never was." Stranger spit on the floor. "You comin' to see the show?"

questionMark

"I should, but it'd be odd, seein' you die so soon after I met ya. Findin' out you're not a murderin' man and all."

"Never said I wasn't," Stranger mumbled, growing slightly agitated. There had been a time where he had seen things from the boy's perspective, but nowadays, such optimism was only annoying. "You're a nice boy," he added after he had given himself a moment to settle down, "and nice boys shouldn't have to see things like that."

"Everyone still sees it, though. Everyone's got to go now."

"Do they, now?"

"Yes, sir. I've seen a lot of 'em. After so long, I heard, it changes ya."

"That it does."

There was a moment's silence between them, which gave Dirk time to think and Stranger time to scratch a sudden itch on his neck. Dirk was the one to speak next.

"Did you really kill him, or did you say that just so people'd stop askin'?"

Stranger seemed to be silent, but if Dirk had listened carefully, he would have heard Stranger mutter, "Happens so often, I forget what I'm doin'." He then looked up at the boy and asked, "You know what I do to calm myself down, make myself at ease when I'm alone on the trail, not a soul to talk to?" Stranger didn't wait for a reply; he knew full well that Dirk was too curious to dismiss the question. "I sing a song. Would you like to hear a song, angel of the Lord?"

As Stranger had predicted, Dirk was curious, but he was also cautious, as his late grandfather had been. "I wouldn't mind it, no."

"Your type would like songs," Stranger grumbled to himself, before speaking up. "Would sure lighten the mood 'round here. Not by much, though."

"What song is it?"

"You wouldn't know it, I don't think," Stranger replied, "but it's a song I sing to myself all the time. I sung it to your granddad when I saw him." And then, after a few chords, the hypnotic voice and the bittersweet notes of the old guitar rang through the air, enchanting a Collinsworth once again:

"He perched upon the rainbow high
Watched the clouds and years go by
Every night, to the moon he'd cry
For the judgment day to come.

A weary trav'ler he must be
Sailing on the open sea
'I will wait, for her I'll see
For the judgment day will come.'"

Dirk sat, not a word escaping his innocent lips. He didn't realize he had been in a trance until Stranger spoke again.

"Good song, ainnit?"

Dirk nodded. "Beautiful."

"I never get tired of it. It's all I ever sing."

"I can't imagine how you'd sing anything else," Dirk commented dreamily.

Stranger nodded. "Well, you'd better get home, boy, 'fore you get too attached to me. You'd best be stayin' at the inn where you'll be useful, 'stead of bein' caught b'friendin' a man like me. 'Sides, your granddad may be dead, but his business sure ain't."

The boy agreed and started to leave after saying his goodbyes, but before Dirk was out of earshot, Stranger added, "It won't be so bad when the day after next comes. You'll stop missin' me after a time."

*

On the morning of Stranger's execution, the whole town was up and ready. Still, even now, Stranger did not tremble, nor did he even speak as he was escorted out of his cell and paraded down the main road to the hanging tree. There were a rope and stool already set up for him; there was no need to waste time.

Stranger stood unmoving on the stool with the rope around his neck. His silver eyes hardly showed a flicker of sensitivity when he heard the charges, reasonable or otherwise, being pressed

against him. Only when silence fell did Stranger turn h
toward the crowd. The crowd of seemingly innocent people who had gone out of their way to see a man die. Like Dirk had said, everyone's got to go now.

Goodwill, Stranger reflected. There's goodwill in this town, alright.

He looked over the crowd and saw none other than young Dirk—good, innocent Dirk—at the very front, even though he was a well-built boy and could've been just fine farther back.

Because Stranger had supposedly killed his granddad. If that was the case, then no one would've let him stand anywhere else.

Stranger cast his eyes to the fading morning stars, thinking back to that night where he had sat with the old man, the diamond stars framing the crimson moon. What a sight that had been. He tried to focus on one in particular so he could numb his mind and wouldn't feel the rope tighten around his neck and the stool threaten to be kicked from under his feet.

He sung softly, as that also helped him in times like this, even though his guitar was still in the jail cell.

> "'We've walked this earth, my horse and I
> We've seen the years go sailin' by
> I long for rest, though I've nowhere to lay
> So on we go without a friend
> For mine's a pain that none can mend
> It's a lonely road towards the judgment day.'"

Singing was comfortable for him, even with the rope tight against his neck. Perhaps it was a vain attempt to mesmerize the people into freeing him, although he would've been surprised if that had actually happened. That was what Stranger had learned over the course of his long journey. People were cold and heartless at their core, no matter how many times they said they went to church and did this and that for the Good Lord. People, all of them, they deserved what was coming to them ...

As much as he tried to tell himself this, as much as he wanted to make his job easier, there were still people like Dirk and his grandfather. Good people. Good people who, had they more power over the situation, would've probably prevented this from—

The stool was kicked from under his feet, and Mr. Stranger dropped. However, before he had the sense to choke and writhe, Stranger hung limp like a rag doll. He hung that way for so long, people had begun to think he had died before the real show began. He had closed his eyes, the only evidence that there was, indeed, some physical struggle. He wasn't visibly choking, wasn't struggling to breathe; if he was fighting for his life, he was a master at hiding it.

For half an hour, he hung silent, stubbornly refusing to give the people what they had come for. An hour passed after that, and there was still no real evidence that Stranger was alive or struggling to live. His body was still, but only Dirk could see the subtle movements of the hanging man's chest. Perhaps it was only a trick of the light, a shadow, or perhaps ...

Perhaps Dirk had too much hope. That was it.

*

It was only Dirk's second night of manning the inn by himself. It normally wouldn't have been a difficult job, but since Ezra's death—and especially now, after the execution of his supposed murderer—the guests had been in a huge uproar.

"Serves him right," one of the men grumbled at dinnertime. Dirk sat on the other side of the table, eating some of the roast he had prepared for them. "He deserved every minute of the drop. It'd be one thing if he was shootin' another gunslinger, but to catch an old man alone in the middle of the night? That's cowardice, right there. Who does he think he is?"

Dirk was about to point out that Stranger wasn't even a gunslinger, but he wisely held his tongue.

"'Every minute of the drop,' what are you talkin' about? He died the first minute in," another man pointed out. "Figures, you got a man who don't care about nothin'. Don't care that he's killed a man, don't even care to put on a show when they hang 'im."

"I'll drink to that," the first man said. It was then that Dirk looked over and noticed that the man was firmly latched to a bottle of gin. He took a long swig before he continued, "Don't care that he's goin' to Hell, either."

"Suits him right."

"'Cause he *is* goin' to Hell, I'll say that much about 'im," the drunk man, only getting drunker, continued. "If he ain't good an' dead, I'll *make* 'im good an' dead."

"Jimmy, watch yourself," the second man warned, but Drunk Jimmy continued on his slurred rant.

"I'll go over there and do it, you just watch me! If the Devil's work made him still alive, I'll go over there an' snap his neck a good one! I'll snap his neck so he's lookin' at God for the rest of his days! I'll go an' do it, don't you stop me!"

Thankfully, his companion disobeyed and tried to keep Drunk Jimmy from running out the door and making his way to the hanging tree under which Stranger should have been buried. Drunk Jimmy struggled against his companion until, to Dirk's horror, it turned into a full out brawl. Dirk tried to stop the fight, although his priorities quickly shifted to making sure nothing in his grandfather's inn was severely damaged. To Dirk's dismay, cabinets were broken, glass shattered, and there were plenty of noticeable dents in the walls.

Fate had it that Dirk was so preoccupied with keeping the brawl safely contained that he didn't immediately react to the clangs of candlesticks hitting the floor. Dirk had realized only a few seconds too late what had happened, and so had the sober of the two brawlers as the fight suddenly halted.

The dry wooden floor ignited immediately, and without a second thought, Dirk ran to stamp out the flames. His attempts were fruitless; the fire was spreading so rapidly, there wasn't enough time to contain it. The guests—aside from Jimmy, who was still wondering why all the fighting had stopped—panicked and did whatever they could to put out the fire.

Dirk tried to remain calm and level, but with sweat cascading down his brow, the flames searing his flesh as they had done to the roast he had prepared not half an hour earlier, the smoke becoming a noose tightening around his neck, he could only shout, "Damn you!"

The inn was falling apart around them. Avalanches of smoldering wood were raining down, exposing the clear night sky now soiled with smoke. Most of the guests had escaped while Dirk tried to salvage what he could of the inn, of Ezra's belongings. He didn't care whether or not he made it out alive—damn it, he didn't want to see everything his grandfather had worked for be destroyed, especially not so soon after he had died. And if he didn't make it, then at least Dirk would be able to see his granddad again ...

Suddenly, amid the roar of the flames, the crackle of burning wood, the screams of the people outside, Dirk thought he heard a quiet, familiar, melodic voice that grew louder and louder, accompanied by the discordant twang of an old guitar.

> "Flowers bloom, and flowers fade
> Of her eyes, they bloom the shade
> Flowers bloom, and he still waits
> For the judgment day to come."

Oh, Lord in heaven ...

However, before Dirk could get another thought across, his mind became clouded. He was dying, that much was clear to him. He was dying, and he was gonna go to heaven now, although that didn't explain the return of Stranger's song.

He barely recollected being lifted up. He barely recollected even falling down in the first place. He felt himself being slung over a shoulder and also brushing up against rope.

Rope? It couldn't be ...

The stench of smoke gradually went away, although Dirk didn't know whether it was because he was out of the inn or because he was being carried off to heaven by an angel who happened to have Stranger's voice. Perhaps Stranger really did have the voice of an angel, he numbly reasoned. Dirk faintly heard yelling from the distance, a much larger uproar than at the inn. The word "Devil" stuck out more than anything. Were they screaming at him? No, they were screaming at the man who had saved him, "Devil! Devil!"

Above all the uproar, though, was a reassuring voice—a voice he thought he would never hear again, and a voice that still haunted him, even from what should have been beyond the grave.

"Don't you worry," Stranger, or the apparition who sounded uncannily like him, gently whispered as if he were holding a babe. "You're gonna survive. I'll make sure of it myself. I've been on this trail a long time. A trail called Earth, a trail called life. I'll tell you why I'm not afraid of death, why I've never been. He and I are one. He controls me now. He keeps me here 'till the judgment day, and I am his bounty hunter. But I control him, too. As much as I destroy, I also have the right to leave well enough alone, and there's no destroyin' bein' done here tonight. Your soul's not mine to take, my angel. It's not your time. It makes me stay longer, but it gives me time to find more deserving souls to use as my ransom. Don't be troubled if I don't come back. Don't be relieved. We'll be seein' each other again on the judgment day, where I hope I'll be walkin' in your direction."

*

Stranger set Dirk gently on the ground far enough away from the inn. He walked to summon his horse, who had been spooked by the fire. The cut rope swung as he walked, the noose still tight around his neck. It couldn't hurt him, though. Not for an eternity. For now, it was only a nuisance. He'd get it cut off eventually, but now, it wasn't important.

A mob began to form, threats were made, and torches blazed brighter than the red moon that had welcomed him here. However, this affected the silver-eyed man as much as the rope did. The horse was reclaimed, and Stranger solemnly began to ride into the shadows.

Pistols were shot at both man and horse, but man and horse were unaffected, becoming eerily calm in all the chaos. Both rode slowly, unshaken and uninjured, away from the mob, patiently waiting for them to give up their riot so that the man's eternal journey could be resumed in peace.

And sounding low over the crowd's riot, if one listened carefully, was a mournful tune played on an old guitar and a voice singing the song that would be sung in its entirety for hundreds of years to come.

> "O, meet me when the sun hangs low
> To the sunrise we will go
> I will pray, and I will hope
> For the judgment day to come."

About the Author

Faryl has always been fascinated with the macabre and unusual, having grown up watching Tim Burton films and reading the works of Lemony Snicket and R. L. Stine, among others. When she isn't writing, she's usually plotting future books or pursuing a "day job", ideally in database design. She lives in Canton, Ohio with fellow writer S. T. Hoover and several animals.

She also skulks around Facebook, Twitter, Tumblr, and *farylslair.com*.